GARDEN
OF THE LOST

D. J. Donaldson

δ
Dingbat Publishing
Humble, Texas

GARDEN OF THE LOST
Copyright © D.J. Donaldson 2018
Primary Print ISBN 978-1-687403230

Published in 2018 by House of Stratus, Lisandra House

Second publishing 2019 by Dingbat Publishing, Humble, Texas

Typeset by Dingbat Publishing

Acknowledgments

I'M PROFOUNDLY GRATEFUL for the copy editing expertise that my friend, Meg Waters, provided for this book. If any of you grammarians out there find something that you disagree with herein, it will surely be something I stubbornly insisted on keeping.

D.J. (Don) Donaldson

"There are many worlds, and we are as unaware of those worlds as we are of being on a tiny planet hurtling through space."
Frank J. Tipler, physicist

Introduction

GARDEN OF THE LOST is a departure from the usual science-based novels I've been writing for decades. One might therefore ask, why not just keep doing what works? A part of the answer lies in the story, which came to me, by surprise, many years ago. Since then, it has never been very far from my thoughts. As time passed, I've told the tale to many friends, and invariably, when I get to the emotional finale, my voice cracks and I can barely speak.

I once told the story to a famous romance novelist and she ordered me to "Stop whatever you're working on now and write that book, because it's magical." Well, I finally took her advice. Now you, dear reader, can see what has been trying to get from my mind onto the page for so long.

D.J. (Don) Donaldson

1

THE WHIP-POOR-WILL THAT had been calling all evening from Bailey Acres packed it in around eleven o'clock. But the cricket jam session in the garden outside Conrad Green's open bedroom window went on until exactly 1 a.m. Then, as if responding to the stroke of a conductor's baton, the insects fell silent. Though he was still deeply asleep, the sudden cessation of their sound registered in Conrad's mind and he rolled onto his back.

The garden remained hushed for several seconds. Something new took the place of the silence, and Conrad's eyes flicked open. *What the devil...?*

He threw his feet over the side of the bed, got up, and went to the window, where he saw a strange sight. Down in the garden, illuminated by the half moon, a little boy about six years old stood on the other side of the old wrought iron fence that had just been installed around the iris beds, each hand clutching an upright. He was wearing a dark cap, pale shirt, and dark pants. And he was sobbing... each cry a strangled eruption of longing not unlike those Conrad had often found himself making over the last few weeks.

Conrad grabbed the binoculars Claire used to identify birds she saw in the garden and trained them on the child. With the added magnification, he could read the New York Yankees' logo on the boy's cap and see a Yankees' pin on his shirt. Wanting desperately to help the boy, Conrad tossed the binoculars onto a nearby upholstered chair and went to the bed. With fumbling hands, he pulled on his slippers, then dropped to the floor, felt around under the bed for the big watchman's flashlight, and rushed from the room.

Conrad hurried downstairs and dashed for the kitchen, where he flicked on the lights and headed for the back door. In seconds he was on the porch, but it took another heartbeat or two before he reached the steps and could see around the big shrub beside the house.

Even before he turned the beam of his flashlight in the direction where the boy had been standing, he realized the sobbing had stopped. So he wasn't totally surprised to find him gone.

He briefly played his light around the garden, then went down the steps and along the side of the iron fence facing the house. When he reached the point where the fence turned to his right, he directed the beam to the spot where the child had been standing. "Little boy, where are you? Are you in trouble?"

Receiving no answer, he sent the light down the fence to the perennial border beyond. "I won't hurt you. It's all right. You can come out. I want to help."

A double row of tall junipers separated the garden from the property next door. It seemed likely the boy was hiding somewhere in there… *if* he was still around. "My name is Conrad. What's yours?"

Still no response.

He listened hard for the sound of someone pushing past juniper branches. But except for a mosquito buzzing near his ear, he heard nothing.

Moving forward, he pushed his way through the evergreens to the large side yard that separated the trees from the house next door. There, he played his light over the lawn, thinking he might see the boy fleeing across the grass. But grass was all he saw. He let the beam of his light travel along the juniper boundary and still didn't see him.

He thought about searching through the evergreens, but the boy could so easily keep a step ahead of him, the idea seemed like a waste of time. And if the child lived next door, he could have headed home before Conrad had even reached the garden. *That's probably what happened.*

Before going back inside, Conrad walked the garden, looking behind any bush or tall cluster of plants where the boy could be hiding, but as expected, he wasn't there.

Conrad returned to his house and went directly back to bed. Though dissatisfied with his explanation of where the boy had gone and still puzzled over why a child that small was out so late all alone, he eventually fell asleep.

Throughout most of his writing life, Conrad would wake each morning eager to begin work, to get on paper all the thoughts that had risen to the top of his mind while he slept. When he was single, he would pull on some clothes and head for the computer without even taking time to shower or eat, so powerful was the force to write. But after he and Claire were married and he discovered how much she enjoyed having her morning coffee made and waiting in the kitchen when she went downstairs, brewing it for her became his first priority each morning. Only then would he write.

Now, he began each day with the horror of his new reality. *Claire is gone. There's no need to make coffee... There's no need to do anything.*

Hoping he might be able to stave off a little longer the empty hours facing him, Conrad remained in bed. But, he couldn't get back to sleep. *Nuts.* He didn't want to deal with it, but the new day had begun. Then he remembered... the child in the garden last night. Very odd. Crying at the fence... And so unhappy...

The fence.

That thought got him on his feet.

At the window, he felt the same twinge of pleasure as when he'd seen the completed installation the day before. The fence was an antique, obviously made by a master ironworker who had crafted the main supports to resemble tree trunks. Those and the other vertical bars were heavily festooned with iron vines that carried small metallic clusters of grapes. Putting the fence up had been a challenging task, because there was very little room between the irises and the perennial bed fronting the double row of big junipers along the rear property line. But Nate Goodrich had skillfully managed the job without trampling a single plant. The fence looked so good that even though Claire couldn't see it, Conrad felt better than he had in weeks at the thought he'd been able to give her this final gift. He was in such an improved state of mind that while shaving, he even decided to get a haircut.

The bedroom was connected to Conrad's study. Before Claire died, that door was usually kept closed so the clatter of his keyboard in the morning wouldn't wake her. With no reason now to keep the two rooms separate, he always left the door open. While buttoning his shirt, he heard the distinctive sound of his computer powering up.

Puzzled, he went into the study and saw on the glowing screen all the software loading. Then, his word processing program opened and the cursor started blinking.

He knew little about computers and had no idea why this was happening. To get it repaired, he'd have to drag the whole damn thing to… Memphis? Jackson? He didn't even know where to take it.

Considering that creatively he was sun dried and barren, and therefore was producing nothing, this was a problem that could wait. But could he even shut it off? He ran the mouse through its paces and the machine obeyed, so he didn't have to pull the plug.

Then he heard the doorbell.

He went down the curved floating staircase to the foyer. Opening the front door, he saw a balding man in his early fifties, wearing a two-thousand-dollar suit bought with money Conrad had earned for him.

"Jerry! What are you doing here?"

"Trying to find out what the hell's wrong with you. In case you've forgotten, you're now four months past your deadline and Lasiter is about to cancel the book. Are you prepared to return your portion of the advance? Because I'm sure as hell not."

Reluctantly, Conrad stepped back and let Jerry in. "You *know* what the problem is."

"I understand, I really do," Jerry said, as Conrad shut the door behind him. "It's tough to lose someone you love like that... unexpectedly, when they're healthy and there's every reason to believe you'll have a long life together. But I'm sure Claire... It *was* Claire, wasn't it?"

Conrad nodded.

"...Claire would want you to keep working. She wouldn't have this hold you back. You're a writer. You're feeling lousy because you're not writing."

Conrad's face reddened. "I'm feeling lousy because my whole reason for living is gone. Don't you get that?" Pausing only long enough to take a breath, he added, "No, I don't expect you do. Jerry, do you love anything other than money?"

"I know you're upset, so I'm going to ignore what you just said. Come back to New York. You'll feel more yourself when you're with our kind of people. This is a pretty little town, but Jesus, it's Mississippi... It's soft and slow and there's no energy, like they don't know what it takes to survive in this world."

"I can't leave. Claire loved this house. As long as I'm here, I feel like she's close by."

"If you don't deliver this book soon, there's not a publisher in New York that'll look at anything you write."

"I don't care."

"You will when your money runs out. When you can't pay the note or the taxes on this place, you'll care."

Their conversation was interrupted by someone else at the door.

This time it was Nate Goodrich, the handyman who had installed the garden fence.

Nate removed the sweat-stained hat that covered his graying hair. "Mr. Conrad, I got the paint for the fence. If it's convenient, I'll go back there and get started."

"Sure, Nate. Go to it."

A lifetime of work under the unrelenting southern sun had etched a permanent serious expression on Nate's ebony face. But as Nate stood there, Conrad thought he saw something through that mask.

"Anything wrong, Nate?"

"That fence... I think it could have been...," he hesitated.

"Could have been what?"

Nate stood there a moment, his mind apparently shaping what he wanted to say. Then, decision made, he said, "Nothin'... I'll get to work."

"Before you begin, I'd appreciate if you'd let that car in front of your truck out."

"Yessir, I'll do that."

While Nate went back to his truck, Conrad turned to Jerry. "As you can see, I've got other things to do. So if you don't mind..."

Jerry's mouth opened in disbelief. "You're throwing me out? After I spent all that time and money getting here?"

"Your idea, not mine."

When Jerry was angry, a spot under his left eye would start to quiver. The more rapid the twitch, the hotter he was. That tic was now on full automatic. He pointed his quivering index finger at Conrad. "All right, I'll go. But you need to remember, I'm not some schlub agent from Dubuque. I'm Jerry Owens. Writers need at least one *New York Times* best seller before I'll even read an e-mail from them. When editors hear my name, they piss themselves with fear thinking about having to meet my demands. And you're throwing it all away."

"I'll keep that in mind."

Jerry pushed past Conrad and stalked out. With Conrad watching, he steamed down the sidewalk, yanked his car door open, and threw himself inside. He rolled the window down and delivered a departing salvo. "When you get tired of this self-pity crap, call me. If I'm not too busy, maybe we'll talk."

Jerry slapped his car in reverse and backed up so fast his left wheels went off the pavement, further flattening some ground-hugging evergreens. Every historic home in Glenwood Springs had a marker in the yard bearing the home's name and date of its construction. Trelain, built in 1872, was no exception. Jerry's left fender clipped that marker, knocking it askew before he regained control barely in time to avoid the brick wall that bordered the driveway. When he reached the street, Jerry made a tight turn and headed for the interstate, punctuating his departure with a screech of tires and two thin plumes of rubber smoke.

With Jerry gone, Conrad motioned for the old blue pickup idling at the curb to come back in. He waited on the porch until the truck was parked and Nate stepped out of it.

"Nate, when you get a chance, would you straighten that marker he just hit."

"No trouble at all, Mr. Conrad."

"You're a good man."

Conrad went back into the house and shut the door. He thought a moment about Jerry then went upstairs to his bedroom, where he dropped onto the big Prudent Mallard half tester bed he and Claire had bought at auction in New Orleans two months before she died.

In the wake of his argument with Jerry, the gloom that had lifted earlier came drifting back, so that he lay listless as ever, staring up at the bed's gathered satin liner. Sometimes, the pain in Conrad's life followed him into his dreams. More often, it didn't and sleep became an escape. Needing that now, he drifted off.

He woke an hour later, sat up, and waited for his brain to sweep away the last threads of his nap. Then he remembered Nate working outside.

He got up and went to the big window overlooking the garden, where Nate was hard at work, brushing quick-drying rustproof green paint on the iron fence.

Conrad let his eyes travel to the right... all the way to the Palladian arbor with the teak bench under it.

Claire's birthday gift.

The plan had been for her sister to invite Claire to Colorado for a few days. Then Nate and Conrad would build the arbor while she was away.

But Claire never got to see that birthday because one night she left the house, intending to be gone a few hours, but wasn't able to ever come home again. Determined that she would still have her gift, Conrad and Nate built the arbor anyway.

Her birthday was cold, reaching a high of only forty-three degrees. But Conrad had put on his coat and carried a small table out to the arbor. He returned to the house for a bottle of champagne and two glasses. A few minutes later, sitting on the teak bench, he filled the two glasses with wine and lifted his to heaven. "To you my love, on your birthday." And then he wept.

The day the arbor was finished was the last work he ever did in the garden. Without Claire, he just couldn't generate the necessary energy.

But of course he still cared about the grounds, because *she* did, and there was no way he was going to lose that too. He had, therefore, turned the garden's care over to Nate, who seemingly could do anything. Now, as Conrad looked out at the new fence and arbor and the profusion of blooming perennials and the annuals Nate had worked into all the beds, he was sure the sight would have taken Claire's breath away.

Taken her breath away... Scowling at the inappropriate phrase, Conrad left the window, went downstairs, and out the back door. In the garden, he found Nate working inside the fence, sitting on his haunches so his brush could easily reach the lower rail. He looked up at Conrad's approach.

"Nate, it all looks marvelous. I'm sure Claire would have loved it."

Nate stood and removed his hat. "I never told you how sorry I am about... what happened. I should have said somethin' long before this, but the time jus' never seemed right. She was a fine person."

"I miss her more than I can tell you. Sometimes I feel like a part of her is still here... When I bought this fence for instance... I had no intention of going into that salvage yard, but it was almost as if Claire was with me, urging me to take a look. And when I saw the fence, I felt I had to have it. Not for me... for her."

Nate appeared to think carefully about Conrad's story. Then he said, "I think what you felt at the salvage yard about some of her still bein' here was real. When a person we love passes, part of them stays with us and part of us goes with them."

"If I could just talk to her one more time..."

"Certain folks say there's a door to the place where they go, but it's hard to unlock. Once in a while, though, it opens a crack and we get a glimpse through it."

"You believe that?"

"I'm just tellin' you what some folks think. Now if I'm gonna get finished here today, I should go back to work. I'm glad you told me the circumstances of you buyin' this fence. Makes me feel better."

"About what?"

"It bein' here."

Though puzzled by this comment, Conrad didn't pursue it. "I'll get out of your way then."

Nate watched his employer walk toward the house. When Conrad was out of sight, Nate put his hat on and looked toward the north end of the garden. Shaking his head at some distant memory, he turned back to the fence and resumed painting.

2

CONRAD'S NAP AND his talk with Nate pushed his argument with Jerry into the background, so he was now able to focus, albeit minimally, on other things, including the haircut he'd decided to get.

While he was backing down the driveway, the malfunction he'd just had with his computer reminded him of something Claire once said: "Updating your software is not just for computers. People need it too." She'd meant that everyone needs to pause once in a while and examine the things around them with fresh eyes. Otherwise, most of life just becomes background noise.

Honoring that sentiment, he paused at the foot of the driveway and looked back at the house, letting his eyes slowly travel over every feature. His foremost requirement for a house was that the facade should be brick; absolutely no wooden siding... And no shutters because they were impossible to paint. It had to be one story so the roof could be inspected from a short ladder, and it definitely couldn't have leak-prone frills on it like dormers. Bay windows sag, so he didn't want them either. Why then had they bought a two story wooden Victorian with fifty shutters, six dormers, and two bay windows?

Because passion trumps logic every time. And as he sat there, looking at the great lady, he felt an immense sense of accomplishment, as though he'd designed and built her.

The biggest trees and the largest homes in Glenwood Springs were south of the town square, along the streets named after U.S.

presidents. As Conrad pulled from his driveway and headed down Jefferson, he glanced at the house whose side yard bordered his, thinking he might get a glimpse of the little boy who had paid him a visit last night.

But he saw no one.

He hadn't met the owners of that house, but as he drove, he recalled he'd never seen anyone around it but an older woman. Certainly, *she* couldn't be the boy's mother. Possibly his grandmother. Whoever she was, she needed to keep a closer eye on the kid.

Arriving at the town square a few minutes later, Conrad circled the courthouse and pulled into a vacant spot in front of a barbershop with a red and white pole by the entrance.

Inside, the shop looked like it hadn't changed in half a century: worn old wood floors, chrome chairs with cracked leather seats, the big mirror behind the barber chairs smoky with age.

One chair was empty. The other was occupied by a big good-looking guy with gray hair and a gray mustache. The instant he saw him, Conrad could sense this was a man with presence. Besides the barber, there was only one other person in the place: a pudgy fellow in an ill-fitting suit, holding in his lap a coat that matched the other guy's pants.

"Mr. Green," the barber said. "Good to see you. Have a seat there and relax. You're next. It'll just be a few minutes."

As Conrad sat down, he glanced at the plump coat carrier, intending to give him a neighborly nod. But the man couldn't take his eyes off the other customer, who continued the conversation that was obviously underway when Conrad entered.

"I agree," the customer said. "Congress has a greater percentage of philanderers, thieves, and liars than any other group in the country save the inmates at Parchman and members of the U.S. Senate."

"Must be hard for someone like you to be around all that riffraff," the barber said.

"It's a trial, Bill. It surely is."

The man in the chair looked at Conrad. "I don't believe we've met, sir. I'm Grady Leathers, U.S. Congressman from the Third District. Forgive me if I don't get up."

Conrad left his chair, walked over to Leathers, and offered his hand. "Conrad Green. Good to meet you, Congressman."

"You live here in Glenwood Springs, Conrad?"

"For nearly a year now," Conrad replied, returning to his chair.

"You're not a Southern boy, are you?"

"Born and raised in New York State. Lived in the Big Apple for much of my life."

"I know some around here still fightin' the Civil War would hold that against you. But I'm sure most folks in town have been hospitable."

"That's true."

"I, for one, am glad you're here. While I dearly love the South, little towns like this need new blood every once in a while. Without it, they become so inbred and parochial, progress is nearly impossible. What do you do for a livin', Conrad?"

"I'm a novelist."

"Published?"

"Many times."

"Good for you. We respect writers here in the South. You like Faulkner?"

"He was a fine storyteller."

The barber untied the apron around Leathers and whipped it off him. "All through."

Leathers got out of the chair and checked his appearance in the big wall mirror as the barber whisked the loose hair off the congressman's shoulders. Then the minion with Leathers' coat helped him into it. Leathers gave the barber a twenty. "Keep the change, Bill." He turned to Conrad.

"I don't know many writers, so I consider meetin' you today a special treat. You can be sure I'll be readin' everything you've written within a month."

As Leathers and his man left, Conrad climbed into the barber chair.

"Been awhile since I've seen you," the barber said. "But the good news is, I don't charge extra for fields gone to seed if they're on someone I like."

"Thank you, Bill. That fellow, Leathers, is impressive. But Congress is in session. Shouldn't he be in Washington?"

Bill put a fresh apron over Conrad and tied it at the neck. "You can be sure he's here for a good reason and that there's nothin' goin' on in DC that needs his attention. He's up for reelection in November, but the other guy is wastin' his time. Folks around here ain't votin' for nobody but Grady Leathers."

"Why's that?"

The barber gathered a shock of Conrad's hair between his fingers and started cutting. "If he tells you somethin', that's the way it is. He don't lie, he don't cheat, he don't take money under the table, and he don't diddle the interns up there either. So how you been doin'?"

"Just taking life a day at a time, Bill."

"I always thought it was takin' us a day at a time... Well, look there..." Bill stopped working and stared out the window. "It's old Doc Marshall. Don't see him around much. You ever get short of things to write about, you ought to talk to him."

"Why?"

"Years ago, he used to be the town doctor. Then somethin' happened and he just gave it all up. Far as I know, never took another job. Just stays in his little house outside town all by himself. Must be a story there." He went back to work. "Got a new book in the works?"

"Not so you'd notice. Can't seem to focus anymore."

"What with your wife and all, I guess that's not surprisin'. You'll find your way."

"I need to... and soon."

By the time Conrad was finished at the barber, his plan to make the day a constructive one had once again left him. So he walked across the street to the courthouse, sat awhile on one of the benches near the bronze statue of Hernando de Soto, and watched the Honorable Cecil Cooper, the town's retired federal judge, feed the squirrels.

After that, he dropped into Anglin's Hardware and wandered around looking at the tools. It was hard to fill a day when you had no interest in anything. While actively working on a book, he never read anyone else because he didn't want their style to creep into his, or risk the chance he'd run into someone who was so much better than he was it would diminish his own gift. But between books, when it was safe to do so, he read voraciously and omnivorously.

Since Claire died, he hadn't read anything. Because technically, he wasn't between books. He was in the middle of *Literatus interruptus.*

Maybe a video…

But after ten minutes and three passes down the shelves at Movie Land, he left with nothing. He'd eaten at every restaurant in town so often he was sick of them all. And when you go to the same place enough times in a small town, the owner starts thinking you're friends and you have to smile and come up with something personal to say to them. But out at the new Food Giant near the expressway, nobody bothered you. So, he swung by there and picked up a week's worth of TV dinners, a couple bags of cookies, and replenished his supply of dry cereal.

Lunch was a bowl of raisin bran. He spent the rest of the day intermittently watching shows on the soap opera channel and dozing in his chair until the channel selector would slip out of his hand.

That night, in his dreams, Claire died again.

"Come on, we're already late," Claire said.

Conrad stopped typing and looked toward the doorway, where Claire was dressed in slim-fit denim jeans, a black turtleneck, and running shoes, her blonde hair pulled back in a ponytail. Even after four years of marriage, he still could not believe this gorgeous woman had chosen to spend her life with him. Sometimes when they were out together, he felt like that wrestler he'd once

seen strut around the ring with his hands over his head, holding up the
championship belt he'd just won. "Yeah, I did it. I'm the man."

Ordinarily, Conrad couldn't deny her anything. Today, however, had to
be an exception. He'd never experienced writer's block, so that words always
flowed in a moderate but steady stream from his mind, into his fingers, and
onto the screen. But occasionally, like this morning, somewhere upstream, a
beaver dam had been cleared in his brain and the story he was working on
came rushing at him almost faster than he could type. You don't walk away
from a session like that.

"Babe, I can't leave now. I'm having one of those days... The story is
coming so fast, I'm afraid I'll lose it."

"Connie..., you promised."

"Did I? I thought we left it kind of unstated. It's not like I even know
these people. Why would I want to help build them a house?"

Claire walked over to him. "Both their kids are in my class. Even if
they weren't, they're part of this community. They lost everything in the fire.
How can you not help them?"

"I don't know anything about construction."

"Neither do I. The organizers said you don't have to. There'll be plenty
for everyone to do. You can paint and carry lumber."

"The best use of my time today is to sit right here and work."

Claire leaned down and gently put her hand under Conrad's chin. "I'm
beginning to worry about you."

"What do you mean?"

"You're as cute as ever, but you seem to have forgotten there are other
people in the world... who sometimes, through no fault of their own, need
assistance."

Conrad removed Claire's hand and kissed it. "I'm just taking care of
us first. And that means finishing this book so we can get the rest of the
advance. Then we can put that new roof on and remodel the kitchen, like you
wanted. I'm taking care of things so we don't ever fall into the clutches of
gossipy bleeding hearts who cluck sympathetically at each other over our
troubles."

Claire pulled her hand free, her green eyes, hooded. "Is that what I
am... a gossipy bleeding heart?"

"Of course not. I didn't mean you. You're above all that. So go... and be a light unto the others there. I'll stay here and work."

Claire reached down and gently pulled on his left ear. "Bad writer... Bad writer."

She turned and walked from the room.

Already typing madly, Conrad called out, "Have fun."

Suddenly, he was no longer in his study. He was being escorted by a pair of uniformed cops through swinging doors into a tiled space where his world was about to end at a stainless steel gurney waiting only steps away.

3

CLAIRE... CLAIRE...

Conrad's head thrashed from side to side on his pillow. Outside, unaware of his tortured dream, the crickets were in full orchestra, their stridulations pouring into the room through the open window. On the nightstand, the digital clock blinked off the minutes:

12:58...

12:59...

1:00.

The conductor's baton dropped and a hush fell over the garden.

The first choking sob drifted up from below.

Conrad's eyes opened.

What... again?

He got up and went to the window. There the boy was, in the same spot, dressed in the same clothes, each little hand clutching the fence.

Last night, the flashlight beam and a creaking hinge on the kitchen storm door had announced Conrad's arrival in the garden before he could see the boy. Hoping this time to at least speak to him and maybe keep him from again running off into the night, where he could be hurt, Conrad went out the front door and around the side of the house. With this new strategy, his approach to the garden was concealed by a tall hedge running from the junipers to the garden gate. At the gate, he'd have a clear sightline to the boy's position and be only five yards or so away from him.

Afraid to turn on the flashlight, Conrad used the glowing moon and dead reckoning to make his way along the side yard. About ten feet short of the gate, he lost his slipper in midstep. Of course, when that bare foot hit the ground, a sharp stone waited for it. He yelped in surprise, but had enough self-control to do it mostly in his head. Forgetting his slipper, he kept moving. Reaching the gate, he flicked on his light, directed its beam at the boy, and called out at the same time. "Please don't run. I'm a friend."

But he was talking only to the night, for the boy was gone.

❦

THE NEXT MORNING, with the wound of Claire's loss freshened by the dream of her death, Conrad got up and went directly into the study. There, he picked up the framed 8x10 picture he kept by his computer; a photo of her in his lap, taken back when they were happy, when they didn't know the end of her life was about to overtake them.

He caressed Claire through the glass. So beautiful... so graceful. How *could* she be gone? Even now it seemed impossible... monstrous... a crushing weight no one should have to carry. How many times over his career had he used the word *lonely* in his writing... fifty... a hundred? He couldn't say. Whatever the number, he'd never really understood the meaning of the word. But now he did. He was a graduate now of a school he'd never signed up for and wanted nothing to do with.

By the time he got dressed, he'd begun to think about the boy in the garden. Two nights in a row... What was *that* all about? Despite his problems, the situation with the child was too peculiar to ignore. He let his curiosity simmer for another half hour, then he walked to the corner, went a short way down Van Buren, and rang the bell of the house whose large side yard bordered his.

After a short wait, the woman he'd seen several times around the place answered the door. She was at least seventy, but it was obvious from her high cheekbones and large brown eyes she had once been a woman of uncommon beauty. Unlike so many women who put on the standard ten pounds a decade, she had remained slim. Her expression was guarded but friendly.

"Good morning. I'm Conrad Green. I live just around the corner on Jefferson."

Her barricades went down. "Mr. Green. Of course. I'm Ann Neville. I loved your last book. All the characters were so *real*. I thought you did a particularly marvelous job portraying Grace Kirby. I should have recognized you. Please come in."

The entry had the typical fourteen-foot ceiling of most other homes in the area, but the chandelier was truly astonishing in its size and the complexity of its crystal garlands. Green marble adorned the floor and someone had done a masterful faux marble finish on the walls. Conrad didn't know the names of the fresh flowers in the arrangement on the French console table, but he suspected few of them were grown in Mississippi.

"I'm sorry to bother you so early," he said. "Do you have a little boy living here or visiting?"

"No. Why do you ask?"

"I've had an unusual experience the last two nights."

"Mr. Green, I was about to have some tea and toasted English muffins. Please join me and tell me what happened."

"I don't want to impose…"

"I wouldn't have asked if I felt you were imposing."

"All right then. But please, forget the Mr. Green. It's Conrad."

"And you must call me Ann. Would you mind terribly if we spoke in the kitchen? We could sit in the parlor, but I've always felt that if God wanted us to drink tea and eat anything without a table in front of us, he'd have given us more hands."

"That's the truth," Conrad replied. "I hate cocktail parties for just that reason… Well… that's one of the reasons."

"It's this way," Ann said, heading for the far end of the foyer to an arched doorway beside the large oak staircase.

In the bright and fully modernized kitchen, Ann went to the breakfast table and pulled out a chair across from the place setting she'd obviously laid out for herself before Conrad arrived.

"Just have a seat and I'll get things together. Go on with your story. I'm anxious to hear what happened."

As Conrad sat down, Ann put a green plastic mat in front of him and began gathering another place setting.

"Two nights ago," he began, "I woke around one o'clock to the sound of a child crying in my backyard. I got up, looked out the window, and saw a little boy, standing outside the iron fence I just had installed around my iris garden. He was holding onto the fence and looking inside at the flowers."

Ann put a cup and saucer in front of him and kept working.

"I went down to see what was wrong, but when I got there, he was gone. I called to him and looked all along the fence, but he was no longer there."

His host added a plate and some silverware to what she'd already given him, her brow furrowed. "How old would you say he was?"

"I don't know… around six, seven maybe, not much older.

"That's awfully late for a child so young to be out by himself."

"My thought too."

Ann went to the counter, sliced some muffins, buttered them, and put them in the toaster oven. "The boy's parents must be very careless. I sometimes think couples should be required to pass a test of some kind before they're issued any baby-making equipment."

"That's not the end of it. He returned at the same hour last night… crying again."

Ann turned from her work. "Were you able to speak to him this time?"

"Didn't even get close. I tried, but it was as if he knew I was coming and ran before I got there."

"Can't imagine where he's coming from," Ann said. "There are forty acres of woods and overgrown field between our homes and those on Adams. It's hard enough to navigate those places in the daylight, so I wouldn't think he's from over there."

"I wonder if he's lost and hiding in the woods during the day and coming out only at night."

"Have you checked to see if anyone's reported a missing child?"

"Didn't think of it."

"Keep an eye on those muffins and I'll make the call."

Ann went to the wall phone and punched in a number. "Yalobusha County Sheriff's office, please."

Seeing that the muffins were ready, Conrad took them out of the oven, put them on the plate Ann had set out, and carried them to the table.

"This is Ann Neville on Van Buren. Has anyone reported a child missing in the last few days?"

She listened to the reply, then looked at Conrad and shook her head. "I'm calling because for the last two nights, my neighbor, who lives on Jefferson, has seen a little boy around six or seven years old standing near his garden fence well after midnight on both occasions. And we can't imagine who he belongs to."

There was another pause while Ann listened again, then she asked Conrad, "How was he dressed?"

"Dark ball cap, dark pants, pale T-shirt."

Ann relayed Conrad's answer. After hearing the sheriff's reply, she said, "That's probably a good idea." She hung up and looked at Conrad. "No one's called them. They're going to send the night shift patrol car around our area a little more frequently for the next few nights and keep an eye out for him."

Still standing by the table, Conrad said, "It's been two days. Surely, if someone's child had been missing that long, they'd have reported it."

"I'd certainly think so."

"I suppose it could be a kid sneaking out at night and going home when he's tired of wandering."

"Why was he crying each time?"

"Maybe he got scratched or hurt in some other way both nights."

"Whatever the explanation, it's a dangerous situation for him and shouldn't be happening," Ann said. "I'm sorry that this child's misfortune is responsible for sending you to my door, but I'm glad to meet you finally. After you bought Trelain, I wanted to welcome you to the neighborhood, but I was afraid that being a famous writer, you probably wanted to be left alone."

"Don't know if I'd call myself famous."

"Well, you are. Let's have our tea."

Ann filled both their cups and they sat down.

"Cream?" she asked.

"Fine as is." Conrad took a sip then held the cup in front of his face in a gesture of homage. "Very nice. I should have come over and introduced myself before this, but when we first moved in, there was so much to do with the house and grounds…"

"I know exactly what you mean."

"And I still had to get my own work done. Then, more recently, I've had some personal problems to deal with."

"I'm so sorry about your wife. I travel a lot and I was away when it happened, but I read about it in the paper when I got back. I sent you a note."

Conrad flushed. "All that is in a drawer somewhere, unopened. I just couldn't read them."

"I understand."

Conrad's eyes suddenly grew watery and he looked at his cup. "It's perverse… You work and work and finally achieve a little success… You find someone to spend your life with and it all seems to be going your way. But it's a shell game, a con to get you to relax. And when you do, you're hit in the face with a punch you never saw coming. Huh… That's a mixed metaphor, isn't it? I can't even do that right anymore."

Conrad looked up. He barely knew this woman, but, in the few minutes they'd spoken, he'd come to like and trust her. He'd borne his pain alone for so long… And then, before he could censor himself, it boiled over. "That's actually the problem… me. I brought this on us."

"Why do you say that?" Ann asked gently.

"The fire that destroyed the Lunt's home... Their two kids were in my wife's fifth-grade class. The day she... the day of the accident, she was on her way over to their place to help with the house-raising their church organized. She wanted me to go along, but I was too busy... had to get my next book out. Too damned busy to help.

"So she went alone. Took the Old Bailey Road. I would never have done that. Foster Pike is shorter. If I'd been driving, we wouldn't have come closer than five miles to that antifreeze slick on Old Bailey.

"But I wasn't driving and she hit it and went off the road, flipped over, and went in the ditch... upside down so she..." Conrad shivered at the thought.

"And now she's gone, and I'll never get to tell her how sorry I am that I didn't go with her. *I'm* the egotistical self-centered ass. So why did she have to pay for my lousy behavior? Better it was me. I'd give my own life, if it'd bring her back."

"But then *she'd* be the one left alone," Ann said. "I doubt she would have wanted that."

"The worst part is that in the last three years, I don't think I told her one time that I loved her. Sure, I bought cards for her birthday and other occasions that said it and I signed them with love, but I never looked in her eyes and spoke the words. Now I wonder if she really knew how I felt. If I could have had just one more minute with her..."

He slammed the table with his palm, rattling the dishes and spilling some of his tea onto his saucer. "No... a minute wouldn't have been enough. I want *all* the years we should have had." Then, realizing what he'd done, he said, "I'm sorry about that. Guess I've forgotten how to behave around other people."

"Don't give it a thought," Ann said, brushing his action away with a dismissing hand. "After someone you love has passed away, it's natural to think of everything you should have or could have done while they were still here. But you can't dwell on that or you'll destroy yourself. I once heard someone say the key to dealing with loss of any kind is to understand that everything is impermanent." Her voice grew soft and very gentle. "Nothing persists. When what we have is gone, we should just remember and cherish the time we had."

"Whoever said that must have been talking about a favorite shirt he ruined."

"It helped *me* when I lost my husband."

There was a time when Conrad would have responded to a comment like that with apparent sincerity, mouthing the right words only to avoid an awkward gap in the ensuing conversation. But he now had a keen interest in death and how a surviving spouse could appear as normal as Ann. "Tell me about that... or maybe you'd rather not."

She sat for a moment in quiet reflection. "It's been a little over four years now. We'd been married for most of our lives and had sold the cattle ranch we owned near Jackson, thinking it was time for Frank to retire and let someone else deal with all those problems. We'd bought this house and had just finished redecorating it when he was diagnosed with Lou Gehrig's disease. Typically, half those who get that illness die within 18 months. Frank's case was more rapid and he only lasted six. When it finally happened, I was devastated. But at the same time a part of me felt... happiness is definitely not the right word. Relief... that's better. Relieved that he was finally free from the debilitation and the pain. Now I know that wherever he is, he's physically perfect again." She looked directly into Conrad's eyes. "And so is Claire."

"Would it have been harder for you to accept if he had been active and healthy when he passed away?"

Ann thought a moment then said, "Yes, I think so."

Realizing that his question could have been taken two ways, Conrad hastened to explain himself. "I wasn't trying to say your situation was in any way less traumatic than mine. I just don't know what to do, and I guess I'm... looking for guidance."

"I understand. But I'm afraid I don't have the wisdom you're seeking."

"Not sure anyone does." Conrad pushed his chair back and stood up. "I'm sorry, but I don't feel like eating anything right now. I should go home. Please forgive me for being a clod."

"You weren't a clod," Ann said, standing. "And you're welcome back anytime. I'm sure on your next visit we can find something more pleasant to talk about."

Conrad nodded. "Meanwhile, I'll practice not being offensive."

—❦—

AFTER CLAIRE'S DEATH, Conrad had put every photo he could find of her on an electronic picture frame that he set up on a small table in the upstairs hallway, where he would see them every time he used the front stairs. When he got home from his visit with Ann Neville, he stood for a while and watched the pictures scroll by. Then, he went to his study and turned on the computer. He opened his Internet connection and typed 'painless way to commit suicide' in the search box.

The first entry that came up was a site whose first three words were "DON'T DO IT." The next site promised to describe seven ways, but also contained the disclaimer that what followed was strictly pitched at people looking for ideas to write a short story. "Sorry," Conrad muttered. "Purely personal visit."

Just then, he heard the doorbell. Despite being irritated at the disturbance, he got up, went downstairs, and opened the door.

"I don't mean to be a pest," an obviously agitated Ann Neville said, "but that little boy... What sort of baseball cap was he wearing? Did it have any kind of logo on it?"

Puzzled at her question, Conrad said, "It was a New York Yankees' cap... with a scripty-looking spread-out *N* and a *Y* centered on the *N* crossbar."

Looking even more unsettled, Ann then said, "Was he wearing anything on his T-shirt?"

"A Yankees' pin—a baseball with the word *Yankees* written across it in red letters and a red bat with an Uncle Sam top hat balanced on it. Guess I should have mentioned those details when

I gave you his description for the sheriff. But it didn't seem all that important. I mean how many kids are they going to find wandering around at that time of the morning? Why do you ask?"

"I'd very much like to see and talk to this boy."

"Why? What's going on? Do you know who he is?"

"I'd rather not say until I've seen him."

"Obviously, I can't promise he'll come back tonight, and even if he does, he's pretty good at getting away. But maybe we can outsmart him..."

4

THE CRICKETS WERE going mad. Tonight, Conrad was not in his bedroom, but was kneeling behind one of the large junipers on Ann's side of the new fence. Just beyond the tree was the spot where the little boy had appeared both times. Conrad had chosen his position so he could see it clearly through a slit in the tree's branches.

Thinking it must be about time, Conrad tried to check his watch. No good. Too dark. His right hand rose automatically to slap at a mosquito on his neck, but he caught himself in time and squashed it silently.

A cramp...

Trying to move quietly, he switched his weight to his right knee, stretched his left leg out in front of him, and massaged his thigh.

Suddenly, the crickets fell silent.

Staring hard through his tiny window between juniper branches, Conrad held his breath.

The little boy stepped forward into Conrad's field of view. He took up his customary position, grabbed hold of the fence, and began to cry.

Conrad jumped to his feet and charged around the tree hiding him, making a considerable amount of noise. He rounded the tree just in time to see the child vanish in a flash of light.

Astonished, Conrad stood frozen in shock.

From Conrad's left, there was a rustle of juniper branches as Ann joined him.

"Did we both see the same thing?" she asked breathlessly.

"That all depends on what you saw."

"You tell me."

"When I ran out to grab him, he just… went away."

"Ran away?" Ann asked.

"Did you see him run?"

"No. I saw him… evaporate in a burst of light. And he didn't arrive from anywhere, he just stepped out of the night and was here." She put a hand to her chest. "Goodness, my heart is racing."

"This can't be happening," Conrad said. "What was in that tea we had earlier? Something new?"

"Are you suggesting that what we saw was a hallucination?"

"What else could it be?"

"Let's go back to my house. I want to show you something."

A few minutes later, Conrad followed Ann into her parlor and over to a grouping of photos on the wall. She took one of the pictures down and handed it to Conrad.

"Don't know why I didn't remember this when you were here earlier. Guess I was so excited about meeting you I wasn't thinking. But after you left, it fell off the wall."

Conrad was shocked at what he saw. The picture was of the boy, dressed exactly the same as each time he'd appeared at the fence, but now standing in front of Ann's house. "Where'd you get this?"

"Found it in the attic when I moved in five years ago. I put it up because I like the connection it makes with the people who used to live here." She gestured to the other pictures in the group. "All of them are from my attic."

"How can that be?" Conrad said. "The boy we saw wasn't more than six or seven. The kid in this picture looks the same age, and the photo's been on your wall for five years. No matter how much alike they look, it can't be the same person." Responding to the expression now on Ann's face, Conrad said, "Oh no… Come on… Don't tell me you think…" He held up the picture. "Who *is* this? Do you have any idea?"

"I believe his name and something about when it was taken are written on the back. It's been so long since I hung it, I can't recall exactly what it says."

Conrad turned the frame over. "Nothing's here."

"It's on the picture itself, not that felt panel. We'll have to take it out of the frame."

Conrad held the picture out to her. "I think you should do it."

Ann accepted the picture, carried it to a small table nearby, and switched on a lamp. She put the frame facedown on the table and removed the back panel.

"Your hands are shaking," Conrad said.

"Gee, I wonder why?" she replied, removing the cardboard filler that held the photo tight against the glass.

"I see it," Conrad said. "What's it say?"

Ann held the picture and the frame up to the light and read the handwriting that was now revealed. "My beloved Felder, taken the day he disappeared, June 8, 1960."

"Nineteen sixty," Conrad echoed, the strain of disbelief evident in his voice. "Jesus, does it say anything else?"

"No."

"I wonder if he was ever found?"

"This is the only information I've ever seen about him. *Now* what do you think about what we just saw in your garden?"

"I don't know… It's too…" He shook his head, trying to clear his thoughts. "You said the picture fell off your wall right after I left… Has it fallen before?"

"No."

"Any other pictures ever fallen?"

"One in the upstairs guest room."

"So this one could just be a coincidence." Before she could reply, Conrad said, "I want to find out what happened to the kid. Is there a computer here with an Internet connection?"

"Upstairs."

"ANY IDEA WHAT the boy's last name might be?" Conrad asked, sitting in front of Ann's computer.

From the small chair Ann had pulled over to the desk, she said, "My understanding is that this house was built in 1871 by the Cameron family and, until I bought it, had remained in their descendants' hands. So his last name was probably Cameron."

Conrad entered the name Felder Cameron in the Internet search box. The results returned no one named Felder Cameron, but turned up a half dozen Cameron Felders. For some of them, all their information was locked behind sites Conrad didn't subscribe to. None of the others was the right age.

Conrad tried again, this time adding the name of their town in the search box along with the boy's name.

"Nothing," Conrad said, when the results appeared. He looked at Ann. "This isn't helping. How about the library? Wouldn't it keep archives of the local paper?"

"It should. But I doubt they'll be on-line. Our library barely has enough funding to keep the doors open."

"What time *does* it open?"

"Nine o'clock. Are you planning on going over there?"

"Aren't you?"

"I may just sit by my front door until it's time to go."

⁂

LATER, AT HOME, Conrad thought about all that had happened. Unwilling to accept what the evidence was telling him, he considered the possibility it was a hoax. If it was, Ann Neville had to be responsible. But there were three major obstacles to that theory. For one, how could she have known he would ever come to her house and open a discussion about the boy in his garden? And, how could she have engineered what they had witnessed at the fence? Finally, what would be her motive?

Despite having no rational explanation for what he'd seen, he went to bed still a skeptic, but a greatly troubled one.

5

"HERE'S SOMETHING," Ann said. She was seated at one of the library's four microfiche readers. Conrad was in a chair beside her. "SEARCH CONTINUES FOR MISSING BOY. Yesterday, volunteers combed the woods and field behind the Cameron home on Van Buren, searching for Beryl and Alan Cameron's son, Felder, who was reported missing two days ago. At the time he disappeared, the boy was playing with a friend in Piney Woods on the east side of Adams. Though it was not apparent why the boy would have left the area where he was playing without telling his friend, Sheriff Penn Rogers said he had extended the search to be thorough."

"Missing two days," Conrad said. "That doesn't sound promising for him. I wish the library hadn't lost the film covering the day he disappeared. But this is useful. Keep looking."

For the next few minutes, as the newspaper images rolled by, they found nothing pertinent. Then Ann said, "Here's another one. CAMERON BOY STILL MISSING. Authorities today said they remain hopeful that Felder Cameron, who has now been missing for four days, would be returned to his family unharmed. Sheriff Penn Rogers admitted however, that he had no solid leads in the case."

"I'll bet he was never found," Conrad said.

"Hope you're wrong."

This time the images rolled by for many minutes without another article on the case appearing.

"We've covered a month since he disappeared," Ann said finally. "Want to keep searching?"

"I wonder if the woman who sold you the house knows what happened."

"Even if she did, I have no idea how to reach her. I remember her saying she was moving out of state."

Conrad abruptly stood up. "Let's go. I know of another place where we may get some help."

———

"HERE WE ARE," Conrad said, pulling to a stop. He pointed through the windshield at a big pair of open iron gates in a tall fieldstone wall. Because of their deteriorated hinges, each gate hung at an odd angle.

"Is that where all the Camerons are buried?"

"If the attendant in the office knows what he's talking about. He said it's the oldest section in the cemetery."

"It looks like it. Did you ask him if the records show that Felder is there?"

"He didn't have time now to check. So we'll have to look for ourselves. You up to it?"

"Yes."

They left the car and walked across the grass to the gates, where they entered and surveyed what lay beyond.

Having had more years to grow, the trees here were much bigger than in the rest of the cemetery. Surprisingly, all the gravestones in the area were partially hidden by knee-high weeds.

"What a mess," Conrad said. "How can they get away with this? Descendants of some of these people must still live in town. Why don't they complain?"

"When most folks remember those who've passed on, they never think beyond their immediate relatives," Ann said. "If this section is full and there's a generation between everyone in here and the rest of the cemetery—"

"Good explanation. But it's sad. And it irritates me. We should split up. If you find them before I do, give a yell."

Heading in different directions, they entered the weeds.

When Claire died, her parents pushed hard for her to be taken back to New York. But she loved Glenwood Springs and Trelain so much Conrad had insisted she be buried in this cemetery. He was sure that's what she would have wanted. And when he bought her plot, he bought his too, right beside hers. He knew coming in today that, if he drove past her grave, he might crack, so he'd come to the old section by an indirect route. Still, it was hard to keep his mind on the task at hand.

Many of the tombstones here were so badly weathered Conrad found it difficult to read the names on them. He, therefore, had to proceed slowly.

About twenty yards into the weeds, he came to a section surrounded by a simple rusty iron fence. The gate into the area squealed when he opened it.

The first tombstone he encountered was an old one in the shape of an urn standing on a pile of carved rocks. Straining to read the inscription on the carved scroll hanging from the urn by a granite rope, he made out the name Elizabeth Mullins and the dates 1872–1898. My Counselor, My Friend, My Wife.

Conrad's eyes left the stone, and he looked far beyond the weeds toward the section with Claire's grave. He stood there for a few seconds, lost in the past.

He came back, once again angry at himself for not going with Claire to the Lunt house-raising. Moving to the next stone, which was a simpler version of the first one in the area, but equally weathered, he found Jacob Mullins.

Suddenly, he heard Ann call his name. Looking in the direction of the sound, he saw her about twenty yards away.

"Over here," she shouted.

He left the Mullins plot and made his way to where Ann waited at a large headstone in the shape of an obelisk.

"It's Beryl Cameron, the boy's mother," Ann said. "Look at when she died."

Conrad bent down and read the date aloud. "Nineteen sixty."

"The same year the boy disappeared," Ann said. "Read the epitaph."

"A mother who died of a broken heart."

Brushing an insect off her leg, Ann said, "I don't think the boy was ever found."

"Here's Alan Cameron," Conrad said, looking at the much smaller stone nearby. "Lost at sea. In 1961, just a year after Beryl died."

"Lost at sea... Does that mean his body was never recovered?"

"I believe that's right. Look how modest his stone is compared to Beryl's. I saw the same difference in monument size over there, where the wife died first. It's as though when the husband died, no one was left who cared about him as much as he did her. Let's check the other stones in the area. If their son is here, he should be close."

They separated and began looking for the boy.

Over the next few minutes they moved farther and farther from Beryl and her husband's graves, finding other, older members of the Cameron clan, but no Felder. The longer they looked without finding him, the more convinced Conrad became that he wasn't there.

Moments later, as Conrad was about to call out to Ann that they should give up, she let out a yelp of pain and bent over, favoring one leg. Conrad hurried to her side.

"What happened?"

"Turned my ankle on something in the weeds."

Conrad glanced down to see what she'd stepped on, and a look of surprise crossed his face.

"There's a place you can sit," he said, gesturing to a nearby marble bench.

He helped her to the bench and checked her ankle.

"I'm sure it's just a light sprain," she said. "It's feeling a little better already."

"That's good. I'll be right back. I want to get a better look at what caused this."

Returning to the spot where she'd been hurt, Conrad bent down and grabbed at a long metal bar. When he stood up, he raised a section of wrought iron fence from the weeds—a fence with the same pattern as the one Nate Goodrich had installed around Claire's irises.

The implications of what he'd just found ricocheted through Conrad's brain looking for a home. But he couldn't allow that. It was too crazy... too disturbing... He needed to walk away... Forget it had ever happened.

DO NOT PURSUE THIS. The warning ran across the back of his retinas in boxcar letters.

But it was like trying not to look at someone with a facial deformity.

He dropped the fence and began moving around the spot, bending the weeds aside with his foot. Then he saw it—

Wanting desperately to be wrong, he dropped to one knee so he could see more clearly. But this only sucked him in deeper, for what he thought was an iron post freshly sawed off at ground level was exactly that.

Feeling feverish and disoriented, he stood up and jerked his head around, staring at all the weeds yet untouched. He'd gone too far. It was too late now to walk away.

He had to make sure...

He set off in a straight line through the weeds, working them with one foot. A short distance from the spot where he'd found the sawed-off post, he located another, and, beyond that, another. He found the fourth on a line at a right angle to the third. Though absolutely no doubt now remained about what had happened, he kept going, madly searching for the next post and the next, hammering himself with the inescapable.

Finally, his shirt soaked with sweat, face red from exertion, he returned to where Ann had been watching his behavior with alarm.

"What's wrong?" she asked. "What have you found?"

"God help me. I think I understand."

"Understand what?"

"Why the boy comes to my garden every night."

Conrad lifted his face to the sky, and his gaze drifted from side to side, searching for a way to avoid what he knew to be the truth. Finally, he looked helplessly at Ann. "The fence around my garden was stolen from here. It used to enclose the Cameron family plot. When the boy went missing, it was because he died... and his remains are still wherever that happened. Insane as it sounds, I think he comes to the fence to be with his mother, to be inside that fence, buried with her."

Ann's face showed astonishment at his explanation. For a moment she was rendered speechless, then she said, "So we have to find him."

Conrad threw up his hands. "I'm out."

"Why?"

"This is not my world. It's some... bizarre distortion of reality. I need to stay with what I've known and believed all my life."

"Conrad, you're a writer. You make up things for a living. Why is this so hard for you to accept?"

"I don't write fantasy. I write about real people dealing with credible situations. I'm sorry, I just can't go down this road."

Ann looked at him kindly. "Conrad, surely you realize... You're already well into the trip."

He washed the matter away with a wave of his hands. "I'm sorry. It's impossible."

⚜

A HALF HOUR AFTER leaving the cemetery, Conrad stood looking out his bedroom window at the contraband fence he'd bought. He'd been mistaken. Claire had nothing to do with its purchase. The decision was a mistake he'd made solely on his own. But now what? Knowing where the fence had come from, he couldn't keep it.

Then, from the next room, he heard his computer come on. Going into his study, he saw, as he had the day before, all the software load and his word processing program open. But this time, the cursor didn't remain in one spot blinking. It began to move across the screen, typing groups of letters that made no sense.

Had his whole life gone mad? He'd never heard of a computer malfunction like this. It was bizarre.

The cursor stopped moving.

As he waited to see if it would begin again, he stared at what it had produced:

P E S H L
US.
DO T E
A RA D

Suddenly, his mind saw something. He turned on the printer and ran through the commands to print the screen contents. In less than a minute, the page rolled out of the printer, and he grabbed it. He sat down next to the computer, pulled a pencil from a nearby holder, and began marking on the sheet. Then he sat back and stared at what he'd done.

P*LEASE* H*EL*P
US.
DO*NT* *B*E
A*FRA*ID

6

THROUGH THE WINDSHIELD, Conrad saw Ann Neville coming toward the car. A moment later, she opened the passenger door and slid inside.

"What changed your mind?" she asked.

"A note asking me to help."

"I don't understand."

"Neither do I. It came up on my computer... The thing just turned itself on and typed what at first looked like a random bunch of letters. But it just needed me to supply what was missing. When I did, the completed message said, 'Please help us. Don't be afraid.' I know this sounds nuts, but the *us* makes me think it came from the boy's mother." Conrad wiped his hand across his face. "Jesus, I can't believe I'm saying this."

"How wonderful," Ann said. "Frightening, but wonderful."

"I still wasn't going to do anything but... If I didn't, I'd be the same jerk that made Claire go to that house-raising alone. I can't be that person anymore. So even though I'm scared out of my mind, I'm out here. What about you? You were willing to dig into this right away. Why?"

"I've lived in the family's home for five years. I feel close to them. Of course I'd want to help. And that picture of Felder falling after you left... Years ago, when a print upstairs fell, the hook came out of the wall. The one in the wall for Felder's picture was fine. So was the hanger on the back of the frame. There was no reason for it to fall. Also, it's a small picture and didn't make much noise when it hit the carpet. If I'd been anywhere else in the house, I wouldn't have heard it fall. I don't use the parlor much, so it might have been weeks before I noticed what happened. All those circumstances make me think that was *my* invitation."

"Believe me, I'm happy for your company. I have no idea what I'm doing, but you seem to have a feel for all this. Why do you suppose that note on my computer had letters missing?"

"I don't know any more about how this works than you do. But aren't you thrilled it's happening?"

"More like dazed."

"I'm not very clearheaded myself right now. But one thing is certain. If we're going to find the boy's remains, we have to focus."

"I'll try, but how can we hope to find him, when even the sheriff at the time couldn't? And it's been over fifty years."

"Maybe that'll work in our favor."

"How?"

"The way things were when it happened, he was lost and never found. After all this time, some of those circumstances, maybe significant ones, could have changed... Different circumstances, different conclusions."

"We should start by talking to the kid the boy was playing with the day he disappeared. *If* that person is even still alive."

"But who was it? The newspaper articles we found never said."

"We didn't get to read the first one that was written about the case. Maybe the name was in there." Conrad fished in his pocket for his cell phone and navigated to the web browser. "What's the name of the local paper?"

"The *Glenwood Guardian*."

Conrad quickly found the number of the paper and punched it into the phone. He looked at Ann. "It's ringing... Hi, this is Conrad Green. I live on Jefferson and I'm trying to find an article that ran in the paper back in 1960. The issue I'm looking for is missing from the library, and I was wondering..."

Ann couldn't hear the other end of the conversation but could tell from Conrad's suddenly disappointed expression what he'd learned.

"No luck, I guess," she said as he ended the call.

"All the paper's archives are in the library."

They sat quietly for a moment trying to figure out what to do next. Then Conrad picked up his phone, navigated to his contacts, and made another call.

"Hey, this is Conrad. Do you have a few minutes to talk face-to-face. I'll come to you... Okay... Where are you...? I'm on my way."

Conrad started the car.

"Where are we going?" Ann asked.

"To see someone who might know the name we're looking for and may also be able to explain the rules for dealing with..." He hesitated, unable to express what he was thinking.

"You might as well just say it," Ann prodded.

"...the dead. Dealing with the dead."

"Who could do all that?"

After he told her who it was, she said, "I've heard the name, but have never met him."

Four minutes later, they pulled into the drive of a two-story red brick mansion with porch columns so thick even a large man couldn't get his arms around them. Already in the drive was a blue pickup truck with no one around it.

Conrad got out of his car and did a quick visual survey of the large front and side yards. Spotting a chainsaw and a red water cooler over by a huge oak that had probably been a hundred years old when Felder Cameron disappeared, Conrad motioned for Ann to follow, then headed that way.

At the base of the tree, he and Ann looked up and saw Nate Goodrich rope-rigging a broken branch that he was apparently going to remove with the chain saw.

Conrad called out to him. "Nate... Hello. Can we talk now?"

Nate looked down. "Mr. Conrad... yessir... Be right there."

Nate carefully made his way back to the ground, where, as Conrad and Ann walked over to him, he wiped his brow with a blue rag from the pocket of his bib coveralls.

"I didn't know you did tree work," Conrad said.

"I'd just as soon nobody knew. I'm too old to be climbin' around up there. But I try to not say no when I'm asked to do somethin'. If I did, might miss out on work I *don't* mind doin'." Turning to Ann, he bowed slightly. "Hello, Miss Ann, I'm Nate Goodrich." He didn't offer his hand.

"Have we met?" Ann asked.

"No ma'am, but… small town… someone new moves in, hard not to learn their name and have 'em pointed out by folks who got too much time on their hands."

"Well, I'm pleased to have finally met you, especially since it's taken so long.

"Yes, ma'am." He turned to Conrad. "What did you want to talk about, Mr. Conrad?"

"Do you remember a boy disappearing from Ann's home many years ago?"

"The Cameron boy?"

Encouraged by Nate's quick reply, Conrad pulled on that string again. "Exactly," he said. "Could we ask you a few questions about that?"

Warily, Nate asked, "Why?"

"This'll take a few minutes. We should find a place to sit. How about over there?" He pointed to a nearby oak with two branches that nearly touched the ground.

When Ann and Conrad were seated on one branch and Nate was facing them on the other, Conrad said, "Ann has a picture of the Cameron boy taken the day he disappeared. For the last three nights, a boy who looks exactly like the one in her picture has appeared outside my bedroom window. Each night, he was on the outside of the fence you installed, looking into my garden and crying."

Nate's mouth was now hanging open.

"When we went to the Cameron family plot in the cemetery, we found that the boy's mother died the year he disappeared—of a broken heart, her tombstone said. While we were there, we discovered a section of fence identical to the one in my garden lying in the weeds. And I found the stubs of sawed-off metal posts all around the plot. It's obvious my fence was stolen from there. The thieves probably did it at night in the dark and mistakenly left that one section behind.

"Last night, Ann and I hid in the garden near the spot where the boy always appears. When I tried to grab him, he vanished in a flash of light. Nate, I think the boy wants to be with his mother, but he can't join her because his remains have never been found."

His brow a washboard, Nate said, "Who else have you told about seein' this boy?"

"No one," Ann said.

Nate jabbed his finger at both of them, "And you shouldn't. If you do, you'll both be town jokes or worse."

"That's what *we* thought," Conrad said. "I told *you* because of what you said the day you put up the fence—that there's a door between the other side and this one and sometimes it opens a crack and we get a glimpse through it. How does that work?"

Nate shook his head and again used the blue rag on his forehead. "You'll have to talk to Daddy Rain about those things... He's the one I heard it from. He's my uncle on my momma's side. But he likes everybody to call him Daddy Rain, so I do. Rain ain't his real name, but that's what people been callin' him for years, because..." He paused and rubbed his chin, giving both Ann and Conrad the impression he was reluctant to continue his thought. Finally, reaching a decision, he nodded and said, "Considerin' what you two already seen, I think you can handle knowin' the why of his name. He likes to grow corn and sunflowers, and even in years when the rest of the state has a drought, his crops do just fine. And he don't irrigate or hand water."

"So sometimes it only rains on *his* fields," Conrad said.

"I've seen it."

Two weeks ago, Conrad would have laughed at this, but today that never occurred to him. "Will he talk to us?"

"He's not by nature a big talker and certainly not to strangers, but if I set his mind at ease about you, he might give you a few minutes." Nate pulled his phone out of his coveralls. "I'll call him."

"We'd appreciate that. But before you do, we'd like to ask you something else. We want to find the boy's remains and get them buried where they belong, next to his mother."

"That's a nice thing to do."

"An article in the paper written a few days after he disappeared said he was playing with a friend when it happened. We want to talk to that person and were hoping you knew who it was."

"I was only ten when it happened."

"Did you know the missing boy?" Ann asked.

"Back then, white folks and black went their separate ways. We didn't even go to the same schools."

Ann said, "Do you remember your family discussing it?"

"My father used to work for the Camerons, so he talked about it some."

"Did he ever mention the friend's name?" Conrad asked.

"Mr. Conrad, it's been over fifty years."

"I was just hoping it was something that might have stayed with you."

"I want to help, but I can't. I probably never even heard the name."

"Maybe if we spoke to your parents—"

"They've both passed."

"Would Daddy Rain know?" Ann asked.

"He didn't move up here from Pascagoula 'til ten years after it happened. I'll work on it... see can I think of someone you could ask. Should I call Daddy now?"

"Please," Conrad said.

Nate punched a number into his phone and waited for an answer. "Daddy, this is Nate. Got a couple folks with me who'd like to talk about spirit doorways. They's local and good people…"

Nate listened to the response on the other end, then lowered his voice, turned away, and said into his phone, "White, but…"

There was another pause, then Nate said, "I know, but that was then and this is now. You need to help 'em. They're on a mission to do somethin' special, and I approve, not only of what they're doin' but of them."

Another pause. "Would now be okay…? We're on our way."

Nate turned to face Ann and Conrad. "Sorry about… him bein' a little chilly toward seein' you. When *he* was a boy, he had some hard years, so now he mostly just hangs around with his plants."

"Do you have time to go with us now?" Ann said. She pointed at the big oak with the broken branch. "We've interrupted your work."

"That limb can wait a while. What you're doin' is a lot more important. You jus' follow my truck."

7

THE HOUSE WHERE they'd found Nate was on Washington Street. When the old handyman reached the end of the driveway, he paused to let another car on Washington pass, then he turned left and headed east, Conrad and Ann not far behind.

"You really think Daddy Rain can do what Nate said?" Ann asked from the passenger seat.

"If you're a fly in a glue trap, you pretty much have to believe in glue."

They followed Nate past the historical Burroughs house, and, a block farther on, the Lang mansion, both of which had been on the 75th Spring Pilgrimage Tour a few days ago. Through this week and next, the town would be a vision of blooming irises, azaleas, and dogwoods—a celebration of life and rebirth. But to Conrad, it all seemed like a Potemkin village—a well-meaning hoax to keep people's minds off the stark specter of mortality that swished unseen through the town's yards and gardens.

Continuing east, the homes became progressively newer and less well kept. Finally, civilization gave way to meadows and farmers' fields. Nate signaled and turned left onto a dirt road marked by a silver mailbox with *D. Rain* neatly lettered on it.

"Apparently the U.S. Postal Service also calls him Daddy Rain," Conrad said, gesturing to the mailbox before following Nate deeper into their expanding glue trap.

They entered a dense pine forest with trees so close to the road Conrad was afraid of losing his side mirror. Then the forest was replaced by a black water swamp with tupelo trees blocking the sun. Here, the road was only a few inches above the water and had almost no shoulder.

"Hard to believe we're only about ten minutes from our homes," Ann said.

"Think I'd rather be there," Conrad replied.

The swamp lasted only for another hundred yards, then the road emerged into sunlight and planted fields. On the right, Conrad recognized young corn stalks. To the left, were neat rows of some kind of plant bearing big leaves crowned with fattening buds.

"Sunflowers," Ann said, pointing to that field. "Now that I see them, I remember... I have a bag of Daddy Rain roasted sunflower seeds in my pantry."

"So he's an entrepreneur," Conrad replied. "Good for him."

"Notice anything interesting about the ground around the plants in both fields?" Ann said.

At first, Conrad didn't know what she meant, then he saw what had caught her attention. "Looks wet."

"And it hasn't rained in town for a week."

"Isolated rain cell," Conrad said. "Perfectly normal... or not."

The fields played out, and the road ended at a rustic home with a long covered porch on the front, a gothic arched window in the tall gable facing them, and solar panels on the roof. Flower boxes exploded with color under all the lower windows, and baskets of ferns and other plants hung from the perimeter of the porch ceiling.

They stopped behind Nate's truck and got out to join him, where he was already waiting on foot.

"Daddy's in the back," Nate said, heading for a path that wandered through an exquisitely planted rock garden.

They found Daddy Rain working at a planting bench with a shake roof over it. He was wearing a wide-brimmed straw hat and coveralls. The bench was facing the cornfield, which meant he more than likely had seen them come down the path.

Even so, he didn't look toward them until Nate said, "Daddy Rain, how you doin?"

"See the swamp didn' get you," Daddy said, as they moved closer.

"Never saw a frog I couldn't handle," Nate said. "This is Miss Ann and Mr. Conrad, the folks I mentioned."

Daddy Rain's face had very few wrinkles, but he still looked ancient, mostly because he was small and wiry and his skin was so thin you could see his skull under it like reading a price tag through a dusty store window.

Daddy took off his gardening gloves and extended a hand to Ann. They shook briefly, then it was Conrad's turn.

Daddy was one of those people who presented a hand and let the other person do all the work, making Conrad feel like he'd just been given a baking potato.

After Conrad had released Daddy's hand, the old man picked up a plant he'd just shucked out of its pot, and he held it up so everyone could see how root-bound it was. "People can get like this too," he said. "All cramped and crowded in their lives… afraid to accept new things and move on to a larger experience. But for some, losin' that fear is the only road to what they need." He looked at Conrad. "Know what I mean?"

"I think so."

"I think you do too. It's why you're both interested in spirit doorways. Come over to the porch so we can sit while we talk."

They followed Daddy through the rock garden to the porch, where Nate pulled the three rocking chairs there into a group, facing each other. Nate then sat on the porch railing.

Conrad and Ann let Daddy pick his chair before they chose. When everyone was seated, Daddy said, "I don' mean to be rude, but I ain't got enough time left on this earth to waste a minute of it. So instead of offerin' to get you all somethin' to drink, we're jus' gonna start talkin'. What did you two see?"

"A boy who's been dead over fifty years," Conrad said. "It all started…"

Over the next few minutes while Conrad told the story that had so astonished Nate, Daddy Rain showed no reaction. "…So we thought you could help us understand what's going on," Conrad said as he finished.

Daddy Rain sat for a moment with his eyes focused far away. Then, still in that place, he said, "There's definitely a door open, pretty wide."

"Did it open just a few nights ago when I first saw the boy?"

Daddy Rain now looked directly at Conrad and shook his head.

Conrad asked, "When?"

"Many years ago. Before the fence was stolen, the boy most likely appeared at it every night in the cemetery. After it was taken, he became confused and followed it, probably appearin' in the shop where it was stored 'til it was bought."

Conrad saw a question form on Daddy's face before the old man asked, "Why'd *you* buy it?"

"It just seemed like something my wife would have liked… She passed away last year."

"I don' believe it was an accident you went into that shop. I think you were chosen."

"Why?"

"It's leadin' you to what you need."

"Which is…?"

"Not for me to say." He looked at Ann. "You're meant to play a part in this too. That's why the picture fell off the wall when it did." He turned back to Conrad. "We're not dealin' here with just one door. There's two. The writer of the note is in a different place than the boy. The door to that place is not open much. It's a progression, you see… The note was able to reach you because of what you saw last night. Before that, your mind wasn't prepared. Once you accepted that the boy was not a livin' person, the note could get through. The missin' letters mean the way is still not entirely clear."

"Do you know where the boy's remains are?" Conrad asked.

"I do not," Daddy Rain replied, getting out of his chair. And I don' know who the boy was with when he disappeared either. "Now, I need to get back to my plants." He headed for the porch steps.

"Thanks for talking to us," Conrad said to the old man's back.

"Yes," Ann added. "It was very good of you."

Apparently, as far as Daddy Rain was concerned, they were already gone.

A few minutes later, as they followed Nate's truck back to the main road, Conrad said, "That is one strange man."

Ann replied, "But he seemed to know a lot."

"What did you think about his explanation of the missing letters on my computer?"

"Makes sense."

"Boy, have *our* standards changed."

"What do you mean?"

"Seems reasonable to me too."

Neither of them spoke again until they reached the highway. Then Conrad said, "I've got an idea how we might be able to get the name of the kid who was with Felder the day he disappeared."

"PROBLEM IS, IN 1972, a tornado blew the roof off the old office and scattered the records from here to Biloxi," Yalobusha County Sheriff Spence Rogers, said. "As a result, we don't have anything before that date in our files."

Even if Rogers had better manners and had invited Ann and Conrad to sit, instead of making them stand while they talked, Conrad would have thought the man looked soft and undisciplined. He did have a cop's inquisitive eyes, though. And they now seemed to be roaming all over the two of them as he said, "Why are you interested in that old case?"

There was no way Conrad was going to tell him the truth, so he let Ann answer with the story they had agreed on in the car.

"I'm trying to document the history of my house," Ann said. "And since the boy lived there, he's a major part of that."

Rogers looked down his nose at her without responding. Then he said, "You must be a very thorough researcher to want to speak with the kid who was with the boy."

"I'm a firm believer in documenting from primary sources whenever possible. The farther removed a story is from the source, the more it gets altered by those telling it."

Rogers said, "Sometimes even a primary source will filter it."

"I suppose that's true, but it's the best we can do, isn't it?"

The expression on Rogers' face suggested he didn't fully agree. He looked at Conrad. "What's your role in this, Mr. Green?"

"We're neighbors, and when I heard what happened, it just piqued my curiosity."

"Piqued?" Roger's echoed. "We don't hear vocabulary like that much in this town. Guess that's why you're a writer."

By now, Conrad wasn't surprised that even people he'd never met in town knew his occupation. And of course, the sheriff should be one of them.

"Certainly have to know words to write." Conrad gestured to a framed display on the wall showing a picture of Spence and another of his father, Penn, both in uniform. Above the photos, a neatly lettered caption read, 'TWO GENERATIONS OF HONORABLE SERVICE TO THE CITIZENS OF YALOBUSHA COUNTY.' "So your father was sheriff before you."

"He was."

"During the time the boy disappeared."

"He can't help you," Spence said. "He's in the hospital too sick to even have visitors."

"I'm sorry to hear that. And not because of why we're here."

"Sheriff, thank you for seeing us," Ann said. "We don't want to take up any more of your time."

The sheriff folded his arms and let his two visitors reach the open doorway before he said, "By the way folks—"

They both turned to see what he wanted.

"I don't believe a word you've told me. Don't ever come into my office and lie to me again."

8

SITTING IN CONRAD'S car after leaving the sheriff's office, Ann fanned herself with her hand. "Is my face red? Feels like it's on fire."

Conrad spent a moment studying her, then said, "Not red, exactly. More like fuchsia. But we had no choice. We couldn't tell him the truth. He wouldn't have believed it."

"Hope I never have to meet him socially anywhere. I'd be so embarrassed."

"I didn't think it'd be this hard to get that name."

Ann turned and looked out the windshield in thought. "There has to be some way to…"

Picking up on her pause, Conrad said, "What are you thinking?"

"Let's put an ad in the paper asking if anyone out there knows who it was. We don't have to say why we want the name. With any luck, it's still early enough to get in tomorrow's edition."

"That sounds a lot better than what we've been doing."

SEVENTEEN MINUTES LATER, Conrad followed Ann out the front door of the *Glenwood Guardian*. "Barely before deadline," he said. "The way things have been going, I was sure we'd miss it."

"Are you by nature a pessimist?" Ann said over her shoulder.

"A recently acquired trait."

When they were both back in the car, Ann said, "Sorry about that pessimism remark. I shouldn't have said that... considering..."

Turning to face her, Conrad said, "Ann, I haven't known you very long, but I consider us friends. That means you get to say anything to me that seems right to you at the moment. No apologies necessary... ever."

Conrad started the car, checked for oncoming traffic, and pulled away from the curb.

Shortly before they reached Van Buren Street, Ann said, "You know, I'd like to see the boy again. After we surprised him like we did, think he'll show up again tonight?"

"Let's find out... but from inside my house this time.

NOT ALL KINDS OF expectations are equal. Waiting for a first child to be born draws on much more of the nervous system than anticipation of the opening curtain on a Broadway play. Similarly, sitting helplessly behind the wheel of a skidding car as it heads for a concrete light pole ranks much higher on the muttering prayer index than waiting for a pot of water to boil. But peeking through a bedroom window, hoping that a dead person will once again appear in your garden is a special category that few will ever experience. These are the thoughts that ran through Conrad's mind as he and Ann sat breathlessly in the dark, staring into the night through the open window by his bed.

Ann looked down at the digital clock Conrad had moved from the nightstand and arranged so it sat on its back at their feet. Over the sound of chirping crickets, she whispered, "Last night he arrived at exactly one o'clock." She pointed at the clock. "It's a few minutes after that now."

"I know," Conrad whispered back. "Maybe he's afraid we'll be out there again."

"The living scaring the dead. That's a twist."

They stopped talking and continued watching. Neither said anything more until 1:20 a.m., then Conrad spoke. "I don't believe he's coming."

"It appears not."

They got out of their chairs, and Conrad turned on the light. "Is it over, do you think?"

"I don't know. Suppose he never came again. Would you still want to continue?"

"Of course. I'm committed now."

"I wanted to see him one more time... Just to prove to myself that this is all real."

"It would have helped me too," Conrad said. "But we know what we saw."

"And now we can't ever view the world as we once did," Ann added.

—✦—

THE NEXT MORNING when the carrier who delivered the *Guardian* drove by at 6 a.m., Conrad was waiting, fully dressed, at the end of the driveway. Rather than toss the paper to his waiting customer, the guy obliviously threw it in Conrad's bushes.

Shaking his head and muttering, Conrad went after the paper and took it to the kitchen, where he sat down and anxiously flipped to the back pages, half expecting their ad wouldn't be there.

But it was.

Now the wait began.

All that day, Conrad made sure his phone remained with him in his pants pocket. As the hours passed with no calls coming in, he began checking periodically to make sure the battery was still charged even though he knew it was.

Finally, at 4:30 p.m., it rang.

So eager to answer that he nearly ripped his pocket, he pulled the phone free. But a glance at the caller ID quenched his hopes.

"Hello, Ann."

"Heard anything?"

"This is the only call I've had all day. But it's way too soon to give up. I've been thinking about last night. Maybe the boy didn't come because he knows we're working on the problem, and there was no need for him to show again."

"Or by being there and disturbing him, we've somehow closed the door he's been using to get here," Ann countered. "Any more communication from Beryl?"

"No. Maybe both doors are closed. I hope not. I promise I'll call you right away if I hear anything."

"I know. I just needed to talk to you about it."

"Want to come over and watch again tonight?"

"Maybe you should do it by yourself. I might somehow be messing things up."

"Not from what Daddy Rain said. But if you'd rather I go it alone…"

"Let's try that."

SO ANN'S PRESENCE had nothing to do with it, Conrad thought, looking out his bedroom window at the night-shrouded garden, where, even though the usual arrival time had come and gone, no little visitor had made an appearance. *Maybe he does know we're working on finding him.*

Conrad got up, turned on the nightstand lamp, and began to pace.

He still had received no response to the ad in the paper. Surely if someone was going to call, they would have by now.

Before Claire's accident, he'd been an optimist. It's what kept him writing during the years before his work was mature enough to attract an agent. Pessimists never survive the hundreds of rejections a novice receives or the many query letters that don't even get an answer. Only the strength of optimism prevails. That kind of steel can't be totally corrupted by anything, so tonight, as he measured the carpet with his steps, a portion of the old Conrad resurfaced.

It's too soon to give up. Lots of reasons could explain why the call he was waiting for hadn't yet come in: The one who knew the name of the boy's friend hadn't seen the paper… Some unrelated personal crisis needed resolution before the call could be made… A time-sensitive obligation had to be dealt with first…

It had been months since Conrad slept soundly. With his mind still in the process of rewiring itself to deal with all he had experienced in the last few days, this night would be no different. Except that for the first time ever, he allowed his cell phone to occupy the place where in his previous life he could reach out in the night and touch Claire.

At 3:05 a.m., Conrad rolled over, bunched his pillow under his head, and tried again to find a comfortable position. In the street outside, headlights came over the slight hill two doors away. The vehicle belonging to those lights proceeded slowly toward Conrad's driveway, but stopped just short of it so anyone watching from Conrad's house would see only the intervening magnolia.

A dark figure emerged from the passenger side of the car, hurried up the drive, and onto the walkway leading to the porch. Seconds later, the shadowy specter pushed a manila envelope through the front door mail slot.

9

WHAT THE DEVIL is that? Conrad thought the next morning as he spotted the manila envelope. The mail is never here until late afternoon.

Then, through the fog of his poor night's sleep, he saw a beacon of possibility. Heart clipping along at a speed more than suitable for a person now fully awake, he darted to the door and scooped up the envelope.

He looked at the front: *No writing.*

Seconds later, the opened envelope discarded on the floor and its contents in his hand, he reached for his phone.

"WHAT'S HAPPENED?" Ann said, as Conrad burst through her open front door.

"Look." He carefully unfolded and held up the yellowed newspaper page that had come in the manila envelope.

Ann read the headline of the lead article. "LOCAL BOY MISSING."

"It's the article we couldn't find," Conrad said.

"Does it…"

Conrad offered her the page. "Read it."

She turned and headed for the kitchen. "Back here where the light is better."

A minute later, Conrad stood on the other side of the kitchen table watching a seated Ann, who was following along with one finger as she read the article.

Two pictures accompanied the text. The first was the exact photo of Felder Cameron that Ann had hanging in her parlor. The second was of another boy approximately the same age.

Nothing new surfaced in the first couple of sentences, but when Ann reached the middle of the first paragraph, her finger went back and she reread one sentence aloud. "At the time the Cameron boy disappeared, he was playing in Piney Woods with his friend Grady Leathers." She looked up. "Leathers... Congressman Leathers."

She turned back to the article and continued reading aloud. "Leathers is pictured above, shortly after he returned from the woods, where he spent an hour looking for his friend, so upset at what happened that he lost his glasses."

Ann looked at Conrad. "Where'd you get this?"

"Someone shoved it through my mail slot last night in an envelope with no writing anywhere on it. So obviously, it was someone who didn't want to be identified.

"What's that all about?"

"I can think of only two reasons why anyone would keep this page all those years. Either from simple curiosity or because it has some personal importance to them."

Ann said, "I think it was personal. If they only kept it out of curiosity, they wouldn't care if you knew who they were."

"I agree. But if it was personal, why give it away?"

"Maybe to—"

"Satisfy a guilty conscience," Conrad said, finishing Ann's thought. "So do you make the call, or should I?"

"What call?"

"To see if we can get an appointment with our Congressman."

—※—

FROM CONRAD'S TIME living in New York, he had come to believe that there are two kinds of people whose residence isn't usually visible to the casual observer. One group is composed of the destitute, who in the Big Apple, live in culverts, sewers, and subway tunnels. The other class is the ridiculously rich, who occupy penthouse apartments or countryside mansions with long, curving driveways that end at tall brick walls.

After Conrad and Ann had gone about a hundred yards down Congressman Leathers' driveway and still couldn't see his home, Conrad began to think that Leathers was more than comfortably well-off. A final curve in the drive proved it.

Ahead, was an iron gate hinged to a pair of huge ornate limestone and brick pillars, each topped by a magnificent carved limestone urn. Just beyond the gate stood a sprawling mansion that looked as though it had been lifted from the English countryside.

"I hope he was rich before he was elected to Congress," Conrad said before easing up to the gate, where he could see a pole with a video camera up high and another down low by an intercom box. "Otherwise, I might start losing faith in the honesty of our public servants."

"State your business, please," a pleasant female voice said when he reached the intercom.

"Ann Neville and Conrad Green, here to see Congressman Leathers," Conrad said.

The gate swung open, admitting Conrad's car into a huge brick paved courtyard with a massive fountain in the center. He followed the pavement around the fountain and paused a few feet from the home's medieval-looking front doors.

"Surely we shouldn't park here," Ann cautioned.

"Does seem a bit presumptuous, doesn't it?" He moved around the fountain and chose a spot that wouldn't block anyone else coming or going. As they approached the front door moments later, it opened before they had a chance to knock or ring a bell. So, they were obviously still being watched.

At the open door, they were met by a slim, gray-haired black woman in a maid's uniform.

Though it probably wasn't necessary, considering that they'd already identified themselves at the gate, Conrad said, "Good morning, this is Ann Neville and I'm Conrad Green. I believe we're expected."

The maid stepped back. "Please come in."

The entry foyer was lit by a massive crystal chandelier suspended from a gothic-arched ceiling that must have been at least twenty feet high. Based on what they'd already seen, Conrad suspected that the scenes of the English countryside decorating the walls were hand painted, not wall paper.

"He's in the study," the maid said, motioning them to follow.

She led them down a carpeted hallway to a pair of richly stained sliding doors, where she paused and knocked.

From inside, a deep voice said, "Come."

The maid slid the doors open and stepped out of the way.

The room was opulent: gleaming mahogany bookcases filled with leather-bound volumes, yards and yards of green satin drapes at the windows, wide multilayered molding at the ceiling. Leathers was sitting behind a burl wood desk so large Conrad wondered how it had fit through the study doors.

As they entered, Leathers stood up, slid his expansive desk chair back, and came fast toward them, displaying a broad, apparently genuine grin. He was dressed in his just-plain-folks clothes: slacks and pullover sport shirt. Before Conrad had a chance to check out the congressman's shoes, the man was standing uncomfortably close to him.

"Conrad, I have to tell you—" He turned and pointed at a book on his desk. "You're one hell of a writer."

Leathers' breath smelled like bathroom air freshener, not offensive, just kind of odd. Wondering about his own breath, Conrad took a slight step backward and asked, "What are you reading?"

"Pressure Point."

"One of my favorites."

Leathers moved toward Ann. "Hello, Ann. I can't imagine how it is you've lived here five years and we've never spoken. Unforgivable of me."

Yet you know she's been in town for five years, Conrad thought. *Obviously, the congressman had done some quick homework since they'd called him.*

"Let's all sit over here," Leathers said, "so Ann can get the stress off her ankle." He led them to a set of upholstered chairs grouped around a fireplace with an elaborately carved limestone mantel.

When they were all seated, Leathers picked up what looked like a TV remote, except when he pressed a button on it, flames sprang to life in the fireplace.

"I know it's too warm for a fire," Leathers said, "but I love the homey feel of one. Sometimes though, it means I have to turn the air conditionin' way up. It's a terrible waste of energy, but then so is a lot of what we do in Washington."

"How did you know I sprained my ankle?" Ann asked.

"Saw you favor it as you came in, and it's a little swollen."

"You're very observant."

"Comes from havin' a daddy with a short temper. When I was a kid, it was always a good idea to pay attention to things. If I didn't, I might regret it. I'm not complainin', just answerin' your question. He was only tryin' to teach me habits I'd need to be a success in life." He leaned forward, rested his forearms on his thighs, and looked from Ann to Conrad. "You said on the phone that you wanted to talk about Felder Cameron. Why?"

Even though their fabricated story hadn't worked on the sheriff, they were afraid to change it for fear Leathers and the sheriff might compare notes at some point. Also, the sheriff had no proof they were lying, only a suspicion. Hoping the two men hadn't already discussed the issue, Conrad looked quickly at Ann and nodded for her to begin.

"I'm trying to reconstruct the history of my home, and since that was an important event in its existence, I'd like to know more."

Leathers looked at Conrad.

"When I heard the story from Ann, the pathos got to the writer in me, and my mind just started to run wild with it."

Leathers glanced back at Ann, then turned and stared into Conrad's eyes.

Oh-oh, Conrad thought, his heart climbing higher in his chest. *Leathers had spoken to Rogers.*

"How'd you know *I* was there?" Leathers asked, his demeanor suddenly grim.

Conrad's pulse didn't know what to do now. It appeared that Leathers was *not* aware of their visit to the sheriff. That was a relief. At the same time, despite the blaze in the fireplace, the room had abruptly grown chilly.

"We read it in an old newspaper article," Conrad said. "What exactly happened that day?"

There was a tense moment, when Conrad thought Leathers might throw them out, then he sat back in his chair and said, "You wouldn't think a man could remember much about somethin' that occurred over fifty years ago, but I still see it all clearly. We were in Piney Woods playin' hide and seek. It was Felder's turn to hide, so I leaned against a tree with my eyes on my arm and counted to a hundred... like you do for that game. Then I started to look for him.

"We'd been playin' the game for about half an hour, and no round had lasted more than a few minutes. But this time, when I tried to find him, I couldn't... not anywhere. And he didn't touch home to win, so I figured somethin' was wrong.

"I called to him, tellin' him to come out from wherever he was, but... no Felder. There's a little creek that runs through the property, and it had rained hard all over the county the day before, so the creek was high and runnin' fast. Because we both knew the danger that presented, we'd stayed away from it. When I couldn't find him, I got to thinkin' he might have fallen in the water and drowned.

"I ran all along its bank, lookin' for him. There was a place where the creek flowed into a big concrete culvert to go under a road, and I was sure he was in there. I edged down the bank to look, but the water was so high and it was so dark in the culvert, I couldn't tell anything. While I was leanin' out and strainin' to see through the gloom, my glasses fell off and were washed away. Without them I couldn't see well enough to keep lookin', so I ran to Felder's home and told his mother what happened."

Leathers shook his head and his expression saddened. "The sheriff sent a diver into that culvert, and they dragged the creek all through Piney Woods and for a mile downstream of the culvert. They tried again the next day after the water level had gone way down. Never found a trace of him. Even though my daddy told me to stay out of there, I returned a few days later when the creek was just a trickle. Course, I didn't find anything, not even my glasses. Probably a good thing I didn't find 'em, or my daddy would have known I was there again."

"Is it possible the boy was kidnapped?" Conrad asked. "Did you see any strangers in the woods or pass any on the way?"

Leathers shook his head. "No. Back then, it was rare to see anybody who didn't live in town or nearby. It's a damned mystery to me where he went. I'd give almost anything to know what happened. He was my best friend. And him disappearin' like that left a big hole in my life. I like to think he's out there somewhere all grown up and happy."

"Of course that's not likely," Conrad said.

"Why not?"

"I think any policeman will tell you that cases like this usually end in the death of the missing child."

Leathers let out a held breath that wasn't quite a sigh. "I suppose you're right."

"What was his mother like?" Ann asked.

"A frail woman, but very nice. She always treated me like her own. She didn't do well after Felder went missin'... became withdrawn and rarely went out of the house. She died about six months later, I don't know of what. Some said of a broken heart. I believe that's on her tombstone."

"It is," Conrad said.

From the look on Leathers' face, he found this surprising. "You went out there?"

"Yesterday."

"You two really *are* interested in all this. Either of you ever decide you want a job, come and see me. I can always use someone with that kind of thoroughness."

There was a knock on the study doors.

"Come."

The door was opened by the maid. "Your next appointment is here."

"I'll be just a minute more."

Leathers got out of his chair. "I'm sorry, but as you heard, I have another meetin'."

Ann and Conrad also left their chairs, and they all moved toward the doors.

"Hope I've been of some help," Leathers said. "If you think of anything else you'd like to know, just give me a call. Ann, you take care of that ankle."

Conrad half expected to see that Leathers' next appointment was the sheriff, but the newly arrived vehicle outside was a BMW, not a patrol car. There was no sign of the beamer's occupants, so the maid was obviously well trained in how to handle Leathers' schedule and not let successive visitors see each other.

When they were settled in Conrad's car, Ann said, "That wasn't terribly useful."

"What did you think of his manner while he told us the story of what happened?"

"He seemed genuinely distressed."

"I thought so too. Did you believe everything he said?"

Ann shrugged. "It all sounded plausible, and to me it had the ring of truth. Are you suspicious of him?"

"No. I'm like you. I just wanted your take on it."

Conrad started the car, pulled around the fountain, and went through the open iron gates, which closed behind them.

Halfway to the main road, Ann said, "I wish we could talk to the current sheriff's father."

"I wonder how sick he is?"

"We could check around and find out."

"Let's do that. But first, I want to take a look at Piney Woods. Is your ankle up to it?"

"I don't think so. You go over there and I'll see if I can locate the old sheriff and get a read on his condition."

10

DRESSED IN WORK SHOES, cargo pants, and a chambray shirt and carrying a flashlight in his back pocket, Conrad stood in front of a padlocked gate bearing a no trespassing sign. On either side of the gate, a chain-link fence stretched along the street for blocks.

Not in the mood to let something like that get in his way, he moved closer to the gate and began climbing, using the padlock for a foothold. A moment later he dropped to the ground inside.

The pine trees comprising the woods were huge and close together with a lot of scraggly brush and fallen tree debris between them, creating a nearly impenetrable tangle, but a vague path led from the gate into the forest.

The path was carpeted with fallen pine needles, so as Conrad moved from the open into the trees, he made little sound. In fact, the place seemed unnaturally quiet... no insect sounds... no birds. The path did not pursue a straight course, but wandered, its direction dictated by available space. That meant Conrad soon lost sight of the gate and became totally immersed in this silent world.

From far off, came the call of a crow, a sound that even in normal surroundings seems ominous. Here, it gave the same impression, but also had the odd effect of making the woods feel even quieter than before. Conrad had no idea what he was looking for, but vaguely believed he'd know it when he saw it.

As he walked, he tried to picture that day decades ago when Felder Cameron and Grady Leathers were here. Were they laughing and talking or were they rendered mute by the majesty of the trees? Then he realized, fifty years ago, the place didn't look like this… or did it? He had no idea how fast this kind of tree grows so really had no way to gauge what the woods might have looked like.

Noticing a couple of fallen trees about ten yards away on the right, he stepped off the path and worked his way over to them. Reaching the spot, he saw that one tree had come down first, then the other had toppled across it so that the second tree broke in half, forming an arch over the lower one. Both trees were large, but smaller than the others in the woods and both were rotting, so they had been damaged a long time ago.

Using a broken branch he found nearby, he dropped to one knee and began scraping the pine needles and other debris from under the near arm of the arch. In a few minutes, he had cleared a decent-sized space all the way to bare earth.

And discovered nothing.

Exposing the ground under the other arm produced identical results.

Breathing hard, he stood up, tossed the branch to the side, and headed back to the path.

Countless books contain scenes where a character gets the feeling they're being watched. Hundreds of films have tried to convey the same sensation, following an actor from afar, foreground foliage or other near object partially obstructing the view. By contrast, Conrad didn't have the slightest notion he was sharing the woods with someone else.

But he was.

At the path, he resumed walking deeper into the forest. About the time his breathing returned to normal, he saw something white off to his left. The trees were farther apart in this area and that meant more undergrowth. So by the time he reached the spot, he was once again winded.

The object turned out to be a boy-sized refrigerator lying with its coils facing up. Despite some large vines that had grown across one end and a stubborn bush with one large branch pinning the other end, he finally managed to work the fridge free of the vegetation and turn it over.

Whoever had once owned the appliance hadn't paid any attention to the old safety mandate to remove the door before throwing the thing away. Now came the big moment.

His heart, already thumping hard from the effort he'd expended getting the fridge into this position, managed to kick into a new gear as he reached for the door handle. Bracing his feet for leverage and preparing his mind for what he might be about to see, he yanked the door open.

Empty.

"Of course, it's empty," he muttered. "What'd you think... they'd scour the woods for the boy and not look in a discarded refrigerator? Probably wasn't even here then."

He crashed and fought his way back to the path and continued walking, now wondering where that creek was. His thought was immediately followed by the sound of a distant woodpecker hammering out a living.

"Sorry," Conrad muttered, "no comprende Morse code."

An unseen twittering bird and two visible squirrels later, he emerged from the woods into a large clearing. And there, fifteen yards away, the earth was widely cleft by a ditch that surely contained the creek he was looking for.

When he reached its edge, he saw only a small stream at the bottom. But judging by the depth and width of the channel, there were obviously times when it carried a deluge. He could imagine how a little boy caught in such a torrent would be helpless against its power.

On impulse, he put one foot over the edge and stutter-stepped down the sloping sandy sides of the ditch until he was standing beside the slow moving water. Looking back the way he'd come, he was now so far below the level of the clearing he couldn't even see the ground he'd been standing on.

The floor of the gully was flat and wide enough that he could easily walk beside the stream and not in it. Directly ahead, the channel curved to the right, so as he set out to find the culvert Leathers mentioned, he couldn't see it. But since he was going with the flow of the water, he assumed he'd eventually find it.

Around the first curve, he suddenly stopped walking. There, not three feet away was a thick-bodied, brown snake with a big, wide head, slowly gliding the same way he was going. Being a New Yorker, he had no idea what kind of snake it was but figured nothing good could come from getting any closer to it. So he crossed to the other side of the stream and picked up the pace.

As he walked, he scanned the sides of the channel, still with no idea what he was looking for. Along his route, he encountered places where the water at its peak flow in the past had eroded the bank so much it exposed roots of the occasional oak growing nearby. Remaining nervous about the snake he'd seen earlier, he often glanced back to see if it was gaining on him. But he seemed to have left it behind.

Walking along the bottom of the gully, he felt like he was in another world, one that was not at all unpleasant... except of course for the snake. Eventually, he began to think about stories he'd heard of people caught by flash floods in dry riverbeds when it rained in the mountains upstream. Even though Mississippi lacked mountains, he made sure that as he entered each new section of the ravine, he had the semblance of a plan for a quick escape.

About the time he started wondering if that culvert actually existed, he rounded a bend and saw a dark circular concrete mouth about four feet in diameter. Approaching the opening, he bent down and looked inside. Except for the first few inches on this end and a small orb of light in the distance, he could see nothing of the interior. He reached for the flashlight in his back pocket and gave it a try.

Now he could see tiny stalactites hanging from the tunnel ceiling like little teeth. But the nearby side walls were clean and smooth, probably scoured by high water levels that only occasionally reached the ceiling. Then, deep into the gloom, he saw what seemed to be a break in the culvert wall.

If the walls were intact, a body would likely be washed all the way through the culvert and out the other end, unless debris had formed one or more partial dams along its course. Leathers said the sheriff's men had searched the culvert. Surely if the body had been caught in a debris dam, they'd have found it, especially the next day when the water level had receded. But suppose it had become wedged in that apparent break in the culvert wall?

They'd have found it there too, he thought.

Wait a minute. Leathers said on the day it happened, the sheriff sent *a* diver in there... *one* man. With the water high, he could easily have missed the cave. Then, what if only one man went in there the second day... and he was hung over, or claustrophobic, or had any other behavioral disorder that made him unfit for the assignment, so that he just scrambled through without really looking around...

Conrad then remembered Leathers saying he had come back later by himself and searched the area too. A kid looking for a kid. What was *that* worth?

Thus, after first arguing that he'd be wasting his time going into that nasty space, Conrad dropped to his knees and entered the culvert.

The small stream he'd been following was large enough that there was no way to keep from crawling in it as he moved. And he could support himself with only one hand because he needed the other to hold his flashlight.

The apparent break in the culvert wall was about twenty yards away, not far on foot, but an annoying distance on his knees. The sandy streambed was largely free of debris, but about ten yards in, he almost put his hand on a crawfish, which fortunately scuttled away before he crushed it. That encounter reminded him of the snake he'd been worried about. Picturing it about to strike at him from behind, he turned to make sure it wasn't there. That's when he realized the space was too small for him to turn around. Even more anxious now about the snake, he bent his head, put the hand holding the flashlight under the arch formed by his supporting arm, and played the beam back down the tunnel.

No snake.

He wasn't particularly comforted because he now realized that the one he'd seen earlier couldn't be the only snake around. Suppose he met one coming from the other direction... or what if a whole den of them lurked in that dark recess he was heading for?

Calm down, he told himself. *And just finish the job.*

A little over a minute later, with the breach in the wall only a few feet in front of him, he paused to consider how best to approach it. He didn't want to simply crawl over there and stick his head inside. Maybe a warning of some kind would be a good idea.

He picked up as much wet sand as he could from the streambed and threw it at the opening. Listening hard, he didn't hear any response. Another handful... same result.

Might as well get it over with.

Sliding along the wall opposite the cleft, he moved into position. Feeling as though the oxygen had suddenly been sucked out of the culvert, he played his light directly into the hole, which began about halfway up the wall.

And nothing happened.

Able now to breathe again, he filled his lungs, exhaled, and leaned over to look into the beckoning cavity.

In the next instant, a hissing demon from hell spit in his face.

11

CONRAD LURCHED UPWARD in surprise and cracked his head on the culvert ceiling. Nearly knocked unconscious, he dropped the flashlight, which went out when it hit the water. Unable to support himself, he slid down the culvert wall opposite the cavity and came to rest on his side, his left arm and lower body in the streambed.

For a time, he drifted in the cosmos, a galactic traveler with no home and no destination. Coming to his senses, he found himself in a wormhole with light only at the entrance and exit.

Now he remembered. *What the hell was that?* The goblin that had so frightened him had beady eyes, a long snout, and a mouth full of sharp teeth dripping with saliva. And its breath smelled like an origami pail full of month-old Szechwan shrimp.

Nearby, he heard scuttling noises.

Worried that the thing was intending to attack, he got to his knees and started backing up fast for the portal by which he'd entered this horrible place. Then his hand bumped into the flashlight. Without even thinking about it, he grabbed the light and kept moving. He paused. Was the creature *really* coming for him?

He pressed the button on the flashlight.

Nothing.

Damn it. He had to see what the beast was doing. He pressed the button again and again.

When miraculously the light came on, he saw a chunky gray shape the size of a football heading toward the far exit, trailing a long pink tail. *Too big for a rat, more likely a possum*, he thought. He'd never seen a possum in person, so he was merely guessing. But its identity wasn't nearly as important as the direction it was going.

With that animal no longer a threat, Conrad crawled forward until he once again reached the cavity in the wall. This time, worried about the presence of another varmint, he kept his cheek close to the culvert wall beside the cavity as he directed his light inside.

No hissing… no sound at all.

He slowly inched forward… Closer… Closer… And didn't see a damn thing in there except some small twigs and leaves arranged in a crude nest.

Okay… so the Cameron boy is not here. Knowing where he is would be best, but learning where he isn't helps too. Maybe farther on…

Seeing no sign of the possum, he resumed crawling toward the downstream exit.

A few minutes later, he knew how the possum must have felt when it emerged from the gloomy culvert into the sunlight. Shading his eyes, he saw that here the streambed and side walls were now lined by concrete. About twenty yards ahead, a concrete roof had been added, making an enclosed channel much larger than the culvert. In the distance and above, on either side of the concrete channel, he could see the rooflines of houses. Apparently, the creek had been enclosed to prevent an open waterway running through a residential neighborhood.

Surprisingly, the entrance to the enclosed section was covered by a grid work of iron. He walked down to this obstacle and played his beam into the murk beyond. And there was the possum casually continuing its stroll.

He turned his attention to the grid work, which had spaces big enough for a possum to pass through, but not a little boy. If all this had been here fifty years ago and the Cameron boy had fallen into the swollen stream, his body would have been stopped by the grid.

But was the stream enclosed like this back then?

When he and Claire had taken walks through their neighborhood together, he'd noticed that many of the sidewalks bore the name of the person who had poured them and the date. He now began to search the channel concrete for a similar stamp. He found one a few minutes later at eye level a few feet from the right side of the grid: Willis and Son, 1983—long after the boy disappeared. Obviously, with no concrete, there would have been no grid either. That's how the sheriff was able to drag the creek for a mile downstream of the culvert as Leathers said.

Blocked now from any further exploration of the area, the whole idea suddenly seemed hopelessly naive. He should just go home. The shortest route to his car was the way he'd come. That meant another trip into the culvert.

Crawling through it for the second time, his mind was focused more on that snake he'd seen than on finding the boy's remains. Well before he emerged back into the light, he'd decided not to walk along the streambed, but climb up to ground level and follow the stream from there.

He had to walk a bit, looking for a place where he could easily scale the chasm's sandy walls. Then, close to a spot where the stream had eroded the bank under a large oak tree, partially exposing its roots, the walls formed a gradual slope ideal for climbing.

As he went up the incline, he noticed a small white object sticking out of the sand near an uncovered tree root. Thinking he knew what it was, he crossed over to the spot and plucked the article from the sand.

A bone.

Knowing a little about where bones of a certain shape fit in mammalian skeletons, he thought the one he held was from a finger. He looked up, under the tangle of exposed roots and saw another bone.

Oh my god… could this be it?

He shoved the first bone in his shirt pocket, then scrambled up the bank, dropped to his knees, and pulled the second one from the sand, giving no thought to the perilous overhanging ledge of soil above him.

This bone looked like one from the spinal column.

Believing that the rest of the skeleton might be just below the surface, he began digging hard with his hands.

With no warning, a tremendous avalanche of dirt around the roots above let loose, completely covering him. This dirt was so heavy he could move no part of himself. But his head lay in a small air pocket under a large root... air that he couldn't breathe because the weight of the dirt prevented him from inhaling.

With death mere seconds away, he relaxed. He'd looked on the Internet more than once for methods to commit suicide, but even as he'd prowled through the sites there, he doubted he'd have the nerve to kill himself. So this was nothing more than what he wanted. And it didn't require him to do anything. *Maybe now, he'd see Claire again.*

But as he reached the end of his oxygen reserves, his respiratory centers screamed at him to do something. Their panic spread to other control hubs, and soon his entire body was in revolt against his quiet acceptance of what was happening. Contrary to his wishes, most of his body, including a large portion of his brain, wanted to live. Commands were fired to the muscles of his arms and legs... MOVE... FIGHT... RESIST...

But the dirt held firm.

The cosmos once again beckoned. And this time, he would not return.

Eyes shut, he began to slide... toward what, he didn't know.

The weight pressing on him disappeared.

He heard a voice... an angel...

But would an angel say "Damn," because this one did.

Feeling dirt in his mouth, Conrad spit it out and took a ragged breath. He opened his eyes. Standing over him was a heavyset old guy in a cowboy hat.

"Mister. If you don't mind my sayin' it, you must be nuts diggin' under an overhang like that."

Conrad sucked in another breath, then replied, "Sounds right to me."

"Didn' know if I was gonna get you out in time."

Still feeling grit on his tongue, Conrad spit again and tousled the dirt from his hair with his hand.

"Thought your friend was gonna get you out," Cowboy said. "I'm sure from where he was standin' he could see you were in trouble. When I realized he wasn't gonna do anything, figured I should."

"I don't know who you're talking about."

"You and that fellow watchin' you from behind a tree back toward the boundary road weren't together?"

"No."

"Even so, what's the matter with somebody won't help a man when the need arises?" He held out a hand. "Ready to get up?"

Conrad took the offered hand, and together, they got his legs under him.

Cowboy shook his head. "Never saw so many folks in here. I come for the pine cones. Use 'em to make animal figures and little people. Don't bring in much money, but I like doin' it, and it all helps. Sometimes I walk along the stream to see what kind of critters might be down here. What were you lookin' for when you were diggin'?"

Now Conrad remembered. The bones... A moment ago, he'd brushed at his hair with the fingers that before the cave-in had been holding the last bone he'd found. So he'd lost that one. Where was the... He reached into the shirt pocket where he'd put the first bone and found it still there. He showed it to Cowboy and gestured over his shoulder. "More of these bones are buried up there, and I thought they might be human."

Cowboy picked the bone from Conrad's hand and examined it. "Naw, this is from a raccoon."

"You sure?"

"Well, I admit I ain't never seen a human skeleton up close, but I seen a lot of raccoons and that's what this is from." He handed the bone back, walked a few steps toward the exposed tree roots, and picked up another bone that looked like the second one Conrad had found just before the cave-in. Cowboy examined this one and held it out for Conrad to see. "Also raccoon."

Though his mind was still scrambled from his near escape, Conrad realized, as he reached for the bone in Cowboy's hand, that he should get a second opinion about the origin of both bones now in his possession.

"You seem to be all right," Cowboy said. "so I'm goin' back to my pine cones. You be careful."

"Thanks for the help," Conrad called out to the man's back as the guy trudged up the gully's opposite wall.

Without turning, the fellow waved and kept moving.

Still breathing heavily, Conrad stood for a moment scanning the edge of the gully, then followed his rescuer up to ground level. There, he saw him moving toward the woods, a bulging burlap sack over his shoulder.

Thinking again about the person who'd been watching but would've let him suffocate, Conrad looked back toward the boundary road and let his eyes explore the landscape.

Nobody there now.

His curiosity about the mystery bystander was quickly replaced by thoughts of where he could get a reliable second opinion on the origin of the two bones.

12

AFTER HIS NEAR SUFFOCATION, Conrad found it harder to climb the gate on his way out of Piney Woods than he had going in. And when he jumped to the ground, a sharp pain shot through his head. But as that pain departed, it left a name behind... Dr. Regal.

Considering how many different thoughts had shuttled back and forth through his mind while he followed the path through the woods back to the gate, it was surprising that he had remembered Regal. They'd met only once, while Conrad was on the Ole Miss campus doing a book signing shortly after he and Claire had moved to Glenwood Springs. He recalled the name, because in scrambling for something clever to inscribe in the man's book, he'd written: *To Dr. Regal, a man with kingly taste in literature.*

A corny dedication, but without time to think, good enough. During their brief conversation, he was sure Regal said he taught Comparative Anatomy.

Reaching his car, Conrad put the long, slim bone on the hood, then for the first time thought about his phone. Did he still...?

He checked the deep pocket where he'd put it before going into the woods.

Yes... he hadn't lost it, but would it work?

The answer to that too, turned out to be yes.

Now he needed an object to put next to the bone for a size reference. A coin would be perfect, but he didn't have any. With no better idea, he pulled a button off his shirt, sat it beside the bone, and took a picture. Then he turned the bone over and took another shot. He did the same with the short, stubby bone.

He didn't have Regal's phone number or his e-mail address, but was able to get the latter from the Ole Miss website. After drafting a few sentences to go with the pictures, he sent everything on its way.

CONRAD STEPPED FROM the tub, feeling much better now that all the grit was out of his hair and had also been banished from the other places it had crept. While showering, he'd harbored a fervent hope the old cowboy had been wrong... that the bone he'd found was human, not from a raccoon. He was so eager to hear back from Regal that he'd taken his phone into the bathroom with him. Now, while drying off, he heard the sound of a new e-mail arriving.

He grabbed the phone and checked the messages:

Regal!

He tapped the screen to load the content.

It contained a couple lines of banter, then what he was looking for: "There's no doubt the slim bone is a raccoon metatarsal. The thick one is a raccoon vertebra."

Raccoon. Damn it. A waste of time.

Suddenly, the test drive with the new Conrad behind the wheel was over. He had his own problems. He didn't need to be taking on the burdens of people who weren't even alive anymore. If the boy's mother could communicate with him, why couldn't Claire do it too? *That's* what he should be working on.

DUSK WAS FALLING as Conrad turned off the main road into Daddy Rain's driveway. He hadn't called ahead because he didn't have Daddy's number and wasn't in the mood to bother Nate for it. This raised two possible impediments to the conversation he was hoping to have with Daddy. The man might not be home, and, if he was, he could well be upset at having an unanticipated visitor.

Inside the forest flanking Daddy's driveway, dusk became a pervasive gloom in which all things unlikely seemed feasible. This sense of unwound reality followed Conrad out of the woods and through the black swamp.

But when he emerged into the sunflowers and noted the season's first blooms dotting the field, he felt order restored, even as, a few minutes later, he saw the interpreter of disorder sitting on the rustic front porch where they'd spoken two days ago.

Conrad parked and walked over to the porch. Daddy Rain was facing him as he approached so it was possible to see the old man's face, which gave no hint of how he felt about having an ambush visitor.

"I'm sorry to just come over here with no warning," Conrad said, pausing at the first step. "But…"

"If you was sorry, you wouldn't be here," Daddy said. "Never say things you don't mean, or people won't trust you."

"I see your point."

"Now come up here and sit. That's your chair right there. I figured you for a no-sugar iced tea man."

A glass of iced tea sat on the table by the chair Daddy had indicated. The ice appeared fresh, as though it had all been recently placed there.

Conrad went up the porch steps and sat down. Confused, he said, "You put the tea out for me before you knew I was coming?"

"No point in doin' that. Go ahead and ask your question."

"If the missing boy's mother can communicate with me, why can't my wife, Claire, do the same?"

"Most likely because they aren't in the same place."

"I don't understand."

"The boy's mother and her son have not reached their final destination because both have unfinished business here. They each exist in a kind of train station, where, once their business is at an end, they can board and complete their journey. Your wife has probably already taken that trip."

Conrad sat forward in his chair, trying to control his anger. "Why the hell would *that* be? We have unfinished business too. I never got to say goodbye or apologize for letting her go out alone the night of her accident."

The old man slowly shook his head. "Doesn't meet the same standards."

"Whose standards?"

Daddy Rain shrugged.

"If Claire has already taken that train you mentioned, how could she have influenced me to buy the fence? Doesn't that mean something?"

Daddy Rain thought a moment about what Conrad said, then replied, "It could."

"So maybe you're wrong about where she is."

"It's possible. It ain't like growin' sunflowers. I know everything about that. But some things about what happens after we move on are hidden even from me."

"Are final destinations farther away than those train stations?"

"Farther and nearer have no meanin' in the spirit world."

"I don't understand."

"Someday you will. Ain't you gonna drink your tea?"

Conrad wasn't the least bit thirsty, but to be polite he picked up the tea, took a sip, and put it down.

"When you came to me the first time, I helped you because you were wantin' to do somethin' noble," Daddy said. "But right now, I'm gettin' the feelin' you'd rather focus on your own problems than help the boy and his mother."

"You're not wrong about that."

"Just exactly what would that entail... focusin' on your own problems? Sittin' around feelin' sorry for yourself... thinkin' about all the ways you could have avoided what happened to your wife?"

Conrad didn't answer.

"That ain't the way forward," the old man said. "It's stagnation... like the swamp you just drove through. You were on the right path when you first came to me. Don't waver now. Sometimes we best serve ourselves by helpin' others."

"Sounds like something my wife would've said." Conrad looked hard at the old man. "You're not..."

He shook his head. "That came from me. But it ain't an original thought. You even had it yourself when you decided to get involved. I understand... change ain't easy... sometimes it feels like a new pair of shoes that are too tight. But they don't *ever* get right if you throw 'em in the closet."

Reminded so eloquently of why he'd agreed to help find the boy's remains, Conrad felt his resolve to do that return, stronger than before. And with that renewal of purpose came a feeling of fondness for the old man. "You know, you want people to think you're not friendly, but..."

The old man suddenly stood up and pushed at the air with the back of his hand. "Now get your ass out of here."

Dusk had passed into night even in the sunflower field, where fireflies blinked over the plants like short-lived stars in a pocket universe. But in the swamp, there were no blinking stars, only a void that seemed lonely as death.

As Conrad drove onto the main road a few minutes later, he thought about how Daddy Rain admitted that Claire might be in the same kind of place that Beryl Cameron was. So it *wasn't* crazy to think, if Beryl could communicate with him, even imperfectly, from where she was, maybe Claire could as well.

Since receiving the message from Beryl, Conrad had left his computer in sleep mode with Word already loaded and a new file open, hoping that having it powered up and ready to go would make it easier if Beryl wanted to write to him again. Now, with the added prospect that he might also hear from Claire, he hurried directly to his computer when he got home and woke it by jiggling the attached mouse.

But a blank screen with a blinking cursor was all he got for his effort.

Disappointed, but not surprised, he went into the hall to the electronic picture frame, which at the moment was showing Claire posing in the costume she'd worn after starring in Swan Lake at the Met in Lincoln Center.

Conrad put a hand on each side of the frame. "Claire, baby, if you can hear me, please send me a note. I'm leaving the computer on and a new Word file open. Do whatever you can to make that happen. I miss you."

He watched the picture change to one of Claire riding a bicycle on a fall day in Central Park. Then his phone rang.

It was Ann. "Are you back from Piney Woods?"

"Yeah, and it wasn't my best work."

He told her everything he'd seen and finished with a graphic account of nearly being buried alive.

"That must have been awful," she replied.

"If I was writing about it, that's probably the word I'd use. Anyway, the old cowboy who pulled me out was right, the bones I found *were* from a raccoon... I checked with an anatomist at Ole Miss. So that whole trip was a bust. Did you locate Sheriff Rogers' father?"

"He's at the Regional Medical Center."

"How sick is he? Can he have visitors?"

"Only two at a time and they can't stay long."

"Even if we could make it there before visiting hours are over tonight, I don't feel smart enough to talk to him right now. How about I pick you up at ten o'clock tomorrow morning?"

13

THE MIDDLE-AGED NURSE who showed Ann and Conrad into the old sheriff's room looked as solid as a battleship. "I can only give you a few minutes with him," she said. "He's very weak." She leveled a finger cannon at Conrad then moved to Ann. "So don't upset him."

Ahead in the dim room, lay a wizened old man with his eyes closed and oxygen tubes in each nostril. He was so thin, he looked like a cardboard cutout of a man under the sheet.

They approached the bed.

"Sheriff Rogers... may we speak with you?" Conrad said softly.

Rogers opened his eyes and slowly turned his head toward them. In a raspy, breathless voice, he said, "Who are you?"

"My name is Conrad Green, and this is Ann Neville. Ann lives in the old Cameron house, and we wanted to speak to you about the disappearance of the Cameron boy."

Suddenly, the sick sheriff seemed to grow stronger. "Why do you want to dredge that up? I did my best. Wasn't my fault we never found him. I was a good sheriff." Then he went on a coughing jag. After it finally stopped, he said, "I was honest and enforced the law equally for black and white. Never showed no partiality for color."

The coughing began again. When it ceased, Ann said, "We were hoping you could tell us what your thoughts at the time were about what might have happened."

"Before me, we had sheriffs you could buy, that'd cover up if somebody done somethin' wrong. I never took a dime... Never. Why are you sayin' I did? I was a good man. I don't need you comin' in here smearin' my reputation. Get away from me... Get..."

He started coughing again, this time convulsive explosions that were surprising and frightening in their intensity.

"What are you doing?" an angry voice said from the doorway. "Leave him alone."

A heavy-set woman in a big flowered shirt and black pants shoved her way between Ann and Conrad and went to the bedside. She raised the head end of the bed and the old sheriff's coughing subsided. The woman then turned to look at his two visitors, who were already backing toward the door.

"I don't know either of you," she said, the skin on her fat face jiggling. "Why are you here?"

"We didn't mean to upset him," Conrad said. "We just wanted to talk about a case of his from before he retired."

In the bed, the old man began to mutter. "I was a good sheriff. Worked hard. I was good."

The woman turned to the bed and put her hand on the old man's shoulder. "It's okay, Dad. Just relax. They're leaving now."

She looked back at Ann and Conrad, who were both heading for the hallway.

When they were out of earshot of the old sheriff's room, Ann said, "Why did he react like that? You didn't accuse him of anything. Makes me wonder."

"Could be he's just out of his head. But if he did hide something back then, how can we find out what it was?"

"I don't know."

"Me neither. I'm no detective. This is way beyond my abilities."

They rounded the corner, stepped up to the bank of elevators, and pressed the 'down' button.

"I guess the ad hasn't produced anything more."

"No."

"Even God rested on the seventh day. Maybe it's time for us to do the same and see if the seeds we've sown produce anything."

"Don't see that we have any other choice."

"Come to dinner tonight. We'll have some nice wine and relax."

"TELL ME ABOUT CLAIRE," Ann said, a glass of white wine cradled in one hand. "What was she like? Unless you'd rather not go there."

Sitting in a matching upholstered armchair across from Ann, Conrad said, "I don't mind." He swirled his wine and stared at it for a moment. "You know how they say beauty is in the eye of the beholder... Well, Claire was a stunner by any standards. Just looking at her made me feel like it was going to be a good day and I could write prose that would make your hair stand up.

"She was a dancer, did a lot of shows in New York until the strain of it all damaged her hip. I always admired how she accepted the loss of her dancing career... no tears—just like you said when we first met. She appreciated the time she'd had and was ready to move on.

"We'd always planned to have kids, but when she was dancing, her schedule was so full, it wasn't possible. After we moved here, it seemed like the right time and the right place. New York is so dangerous for kids, adults too, if you're not savvy. But here, we thought, a kid has a chance to grow up and find themselves without outside interference. We were trying to make that happen when..."

He paused, struggling with the words. Then he said, "She died. Why do I still have trouble saying that? She died, and now I'm alone and can't write."

"Frank and I wanted children," Ann said. "But I had a miscarriage when I was twenty-seven and something in my system was damaged, so we never got another chance."

"Did you consider adopting?"

"It wasn't a possibility for Frank. He was a big believer in genes and worried that even in an open adoption, there's no way you can learn everything about the birth parents. So, in Frank's mind, you can't tell what you're getting. The uncertainty didn't bother me, but I loved Frank and I didn't want to push him into something he was uncomfortable with. I can't count the number of times I cried over our lost baby. I didn't let Frank know, but that pain never went away. I still carry it."

"I guess you and Beryl Cameron have a lot in common."

"I feel very close to her. That's probably why. But in my case, I knew after my miscarriage there was no hope for that child. But with Beryl, she never knew. I'm sure that for days afterward, she believed every morning this was the day her son would be found… tired and hungry maybe, but safe.

"As the weeks passed, the doubts would have begun, mixing with the optimism a mother has to have in a situation like that. Then, gradually, her doubts would have replaced the hope like a cancer. And she would have felt so terrible, not just for the loss of her son, but at the feeling of disloyalty her skepticism was producing."

Conrad said, "That epitaph on Beryl's tombstone… about dying of a broken heart. Everybody's heard the phrase at some time in their life. Before I lost Claire, I thought it was just a line some poet came up with because it sounded good. Now I get it. Oh, how I get it."

By unspoken agreement between them, the conversation took a hiatus while both sipped their wine and reflected on what had been said.

It was Conrad who ended the silence. "In all we've done so far, we've had only one hint that we were close to learning something significant—the old sheriff's reaction to us in the hospital. We need to follow up on that."

"Have you thought of a way?"

"He's so disconnected and confused, we might be able to make that work for us if we could get back with him tonight."

"It's late," Ann said. "Visiting hours are probably over."

"That's good. We don't want to run into his daughter again, or his son."

"I don't think they make immediate family observe visiting hours. If either of them wanted to stay the night with their father, they could."

"Even so, now seems our best shot at catching him alone."

"What are you going to tell the duty nurses?"

"I'm hoping to avoid them. If we can't, I'll say we're out-of-state relatives who just arrived in town and are so distraught we have to see him right now."

"Think I'll let you do this by yourself. Your chances of slipping in unobserved would be better without me."

"You sure?"

"It'll be best."

"What was his first name?"

"Penn."

Moments later, Conrad stepped off Ann's front porch, moved briskly to the sidewalk bordering the street, then walked down to the corner and turned toward his own home.

Two houses behind him, on the opposite side of the street, the driver of a black car holding two shadowy occupants started the car's engine. The vehicle sat idling at the curb, lights off, until Conrad was within a few feet of his front walkway. Then, with only the black vehicle's running lights on, the driver pulled away from the curb and came down the street. With his thoughts on his impending visit to Penn Rogers, Conrad was only dimly aware of a car behind him. So he likewise had no idea it was creeping across the centerline toward his side of the street.

A couple walking an Irish Setter came over the hill ahead. At the same instant that Conrad saw them, the car behind him flicked on its lights, returned to the correct side of the street, and sped away. Fully cognizant of the vehicle for the first time, Conrad noticed that the license plate was obscured by mud.

14

CONRAD OPENED THE stairwell door and checked in both directions.

Nursing station to his left... empty. So far so good.

That landmark told him immediately where he was. He looked the other way and saw the bank of elevators he and Ann had taken on their earlier visit. Penn Rogers' room was past the elevators and down the left arm of the intersecting hallway. Now... could he get there unseen?

Heart clipping along like a kid's bicycle with a playing card in the spokes, he made his way toward the elevators, staying close to the opposite wall. As he headed toward his goal, he mentally saw nurses everywhere... stepping off the elevator... coming around either corner ahead... emerging from some room behind the nursing station. He had his out-of-state relative story ready, but wasn't sure he could tell it convincingly.

As he approached the elevators, he looked at the indicator lights above each one.

Oh crap. The middle one was on its way up and would arrive at any second. He crossed over to that side of the hall and scurried to the turn toward Rogers' room. There, he stood for two thudding heartbeats, first looking to the right, where his view of the connecting hallway was so clear he could easily have been seen by anyone in it.

But it was empty.

A quick peek around the corner to his left made him begin to think he should be in a casino, because his luck was that good. As he darted into the final leg of his infiltration of the ward, he heard the elevator doors open.

Rogers' room was four numbers down on the right. Hearing voices coming from the direction of the elevators he sprinted for the room and slipped inside, hoping no surprises awaited.

The room was lit only by a dim nightlight, so Conrad had to wait a moment for his eyes to adapt. As they did... *Damn it!*

Someone was sitting on the vinyl sofa against the wall beyond the old man's bed.

He cringed, waiting for the angry questions to begin. But no interrogation or movement came from the sofa. Another few seconds and he realized the person he'd seen was a stack of pillows and medical paraphernalia.

As his nervous system slipped from panic mode into a state of mild anxiety, he turned his attention to the bed, where the hiss and sigh of Penn Rogers' obstructed breathing showed that the old man was still alive. Able now to see well enough that he wouldn't blunder into anything, he went to a nightstand by the bed. There, he removed a small lamp and put it on the floor. Then, he pulled the visitor's chair close to the bed and sat down.

"Penn... Wake up..." he crooned softly. "Penn..."

The old sheriff's breathing continued at the same rhythm, and he remained motionless.

This time, Conrad spoke a little louder. "Penn Rogers... Wake up, Penn... We need to talk."

The old man's breathing became irregular, and it looked like he opened his eyes. He turned his head in Conrad's direction. "Who is it? Who's there?"

Rogers reached for his lamp, and his breathing became labored with the effort.

"Where's my lamp?"

"We don't need that," Conrad said. "I understand someone came here today asking about the Cameron boy, and that worries me."

"Oh, it's you, Doctor Marshall. It's true... a man and a woman. But I didn't tell 'em anything, and I never will. You don't have to worry about that. I keep my word. But Lord, I wish I'd never given it. It'd be better for me if you and I had never met."

Suddenly, light from the hallway flooded the room as the door opened. "Who are you?" a voice said. "Visiting hours are over."

Conrad turned to see a slightly-built nurse with a stethoscope draped over her neck. Though she didn't look as tough as either the one he and Ann had met earlier in the day or the old sheriff's daughter, he didn't want to test her. Besides, he'd already been well paid for his trip.

"I know," he said. "I was just worried about him. I'll go now."

Conrad was generally an observant man. It was a skill he'd developed so he'd have a store of material he could draw on when he was writing. But even if his mind hadn't been running at full throttle, thinking about the implications of what Penn Rogers had just said, he probably wouldn't have noticed that, as he walked to his car and got in, he was being watched.

The two men doing the watching had unscrewed the utility plate at the base of the nearest light pole and cut the wires so that their car sat in deep shadow. When Conrad reached the parking lot exit and turned onto the main road, they followed.

ANN OPENED HER front door, and Conrad rushed inside. "I did it. Got to talk to him. And he *does* know something. He couldn't tell who I was because I was sitting in the dark. So I pretended to be someone who already knew what happened. I told him I was worried about us coming to see him earlier, and he said I shouldn't worry because he didn't tell us anything. He called me Doctor Marshall."

"I know that name," Ann said. "He was the town doctor a long time ago. The gossip is that one day, he just gave up his practice. No one seems to know why. I think he still lives around here."

"He does. I sort of saw him a few days ago through the barbershop window. The barber said he lives out in the country."

"Should we try to talk to him?"

"Unless you've got a better idea on how to proceed."

"Obviously, there's been a cover-up of some kind," Ann said. "That being the case, he could be dangerous."

Not trying to hide his surprise at her comment, Conrad said, "He must be over eighty years old."

"Doesn't take much strength to fire a gun."

"Surely their secret isn't *that* dark."

"At this point, we can't say. Maybe we should just tell Sheriff Rogers about what you've learned. Let *him* follow up."

"Then he's going to want to know everything. Are you prepared to tell him why we became involved in this? I'm not. You saw him… He already knows we lied to him before. He'll demand every detail, and if we shade the truth at all, I think he'll catch us at it. And I sure don't want to be the one to tell him about his father."

Ann nodded. "You're right."

"I've got a .38 at home that I bought when we lived in New York. When I talk to Marshall, I'll take that along."

"You shouldn't go alone."

"This is a big step beyond the kind of thing we've been doing. It could be in your best interest to let me take care of it."

"We've come this far together. I'm not going to slip into the background now."

"All right. We'll go tomorrow. Once we find out where he lives, here's a way we can handle it…"

Conrad explained his plan, then said, "I expect it won't be easy for either of us to get much sleep tonight but we should try. Tomorrow morning, I'll call the barbershop when it opens and ask about him."

"I'll check around too, just in case."

Conrad had gone directly from the hospital to Ann's house. After their discussion about Marshall, he drove home and parked under Trelain's big side portico. Both he and Claire loved the view of their home's staircase from the front entrance, so whenever they returned from even a trip to the grocery store, they always went inside by that door. Conrad had continued that practice.

As he slid his key into the front door lock, his mind kept examining his earlier conversation with the old sheriff, turning it over and over like a barnacle-encrusted treasure from an old sea wreck. Believing Conrad was Doc Marshall, Rogers had told him not to worry... that whatever secret they had between them was safe because Rogers always kept his word. He'd made it sound like Marshall was the lead actor in whatever had happened. Suppose—

Conrad never got to complete his thought because a dark figure suddenly burst from behind a tall shrub and darted up the porch steps. Turning to see what the hell was going on, Conrad got a brief glimpse of a face distorted by a pantyhose mask. Then pain... his eyes... Through the agony, Conrad realized he'd been Maced.

Blinded by the chemical, he didn't see the second assailant materialize from the shrub on the other side of the porch. Nor did he hear that one's feet hitting the porch steps. His arms were forced to his sides and held there at first by someone's hands. Accompanied by the sound of what surely was duct tape coming off a roll, his arms were bound in place. Though confused and in pain, he realized that one person alone couldn't have held his arms and worked the tape too.

Furious at what was happening, he opened his mouth and shouted a guttural epithet that was cut short by a rag shoved into his mouth. Then he felt some sort of rough fabric being pulled over his head from behind.

Unable to do anything else, Conrad kicked at whoever was in front of him. But he connected with nothing. A backward kick produced the same result. Arms suddenly grabbed his thighs... a blunt object hit him in the stomach. Then he was off his feet. He heard more tape, and felt his legs being bound at the ankles.

"Finished," a deep voice said, softly.

Now he was bouncing, most likely being carried over a shoulder like a sack of sand. There came three big jolts, apparently the porch steps. A succession of jiggling movements followed, doubtlessly caused by quick strides, probably taking him to the street out front. His eyes were still on fire, and he could do nothing about it.

The same deep voice, clearly coming from behind the one carrying him said, "We got him."

Conrad's confusion about who the recipient of that advice might be was soon answered by the sound of a car pulling up close and pausing with the engine still running.

The click of a latch followed by a squeak, and Conrad was dropped hard onto his side. The slam of a lid told him he was now in the car's trunk. At that moment, he doubted he would emerge alive from this.

15

WITH HIS HANDS BOUND, Conrad couldn't get the rag out of his mouth. That meant he could breathe only through his nose. Impeded by the fabric covering his head, the musty airflow was barely sufficient to keep him conscious. There was no way to judge how long he'd been in the trunk, but he did realize that the car had been moving the entire time. Throughout most of the trip the road had been smooth, but a short time ago, the sound of the high-pitched hum of the vehicle's tires on the road had stopped as its speed slowed. At the same time, he felt it swerve. Then the jostling began, so that he was tossed from side to side like a marionette. Whatever his ultimate fate was to be, it would happen soon.

The car stopped moving. Doors opened and slammed shut. The trunk lid was thrown open, allowing a surge of fresh air through the weave of his fabric shroud. Hands grabbed at him, pulling him from the trunk.

He was yanked into a stumbling walk. At first it was as dark as the trunk, then strong light pierced the fabric covering his eyes. His legs were forced to buckle by pressure behind his knees.

From in front of him, a raspy voice said, "Listen up. We don't need your kind in this town. So take your Jew ass back where you came from. And here's somethin' to show you how serious we are."

A vicious blow struck Conrad so hard in the right temple he crumpled to the ground on his side. This was followed by a kick in the stomach that rolled him onto his back.

"You gettin' the message, Jew boy?" raspy voice said.

A jolt from the tip of a shoe or boot hit him in the ribs, making him feel as though he'd been punched then squeezed by a huge, fiery hand. Another crushing impact accompanied by a grunt from its author hit his ribs from the other side as the second assailant joined in. They each blasted him again, then raspy voice said, "You need to think seriously about what just happened here. And when you do, I'm sure you'll see you ought to move on. I wouldn't bother stayin' 'til you can sell your house. Let somebody else handle that. You also shouldn't take too long to pack. Because we'll be watchin'. And next time we won't be so gentle."

Conrad hadn't heard anything after "sell your house," because he had passed out.

CONRAD WOKE TO THE thin light of dawn filtering through his hood. At the same time, he heard the sound of machinery rattling and coughing not far away.

His eyes still burned, the side of his head throbbed, and his ribs cursed him for every breath he took, yet he still tried to shout for help. But the rag in his mouth, which by now felt many times larger than it had initially, prevented the production of any useful sound.

The machine was getting closer every second. Clearly, whoever was operating it would notice him. If he'd been meant to die, he would have perished in that cave-in at Piney Woods. No, this was not to be his end. He still had to find that boy.

But then, instead of getting louder, the machine seemed to be moving away from him. Surely not. If he was still there when the sun fully rose, he would likely not survive another day. That couldn't be. He was *needed*.

As seconds passed, the sound did indeed grow fainter, until he lost any hope that it would lead to his rescue.

He felt the sun beginning to heat his clothing. Inside the shroud, the atmosphere was thickening so that the pain-limited rise and fall of his chest was barely sufficient to move the oppressively heavy air in and out of his lungs. He could not last much longer under these conditions... not much...

Now on the verge of passing once more into insensibility, Conrad's heart began to beat in his ears making even the earth under him vibrate. He was floating... and being needed was no longer important. He would just go away and... be... with...

Suddenly, his head came up off the soil and the shroud was pulled off. "What in the Sam Hill happened to you?" a sun-weathered face with a straw hat perched above hoary eyebrows asked.

⁂

"THERE WERE AT LEAST three of them," Conrad said, from his hospital bed. He had a huge bruise on the side of his head, and his eyes were still inflamed from the Mace. His lips were dry and scaly and his ribs, two of which were cracked, hurt like hell. He'd been found by Homer Lambert, owner of the cornfield where the thugs had left him.

"Could you identify any of them if you saw them again?" the current Sheriff Rogers asked.

"It all happened so fast," Conrad said. "And the only one I got a look at was wearing a panty-hose mask."

"They say anything?"

"Seemed to think I was Jewish. Wanted me to move back to New York."

"So you're *not* Jewish..."

"No."

"Well, I think we have to proceed as though you are... because *they* believed it. That makes this a new deal. In the past we've had this kind of thing happen to an occasional black person, but we've never had anybody like you... like they *think* you are, messed with. There's a Jewish family lives over on Linden and they never had any problems. Hope this isn't the start of somethin'. Because I just don't need it. What are your plans?"

"You mean am I leaving? I don't know."

"Course that's up to you, but I should warn you, we got a few bad apples around here. I can't in all honesty guarantee your safety if you decide to stick around, even if we get the newspaper to include the fact you're not Jewish when they run the account of what happened. I'm not proud of that, but it's the truth. Problem is, I just don't have much to work with."

"Conrad… how you feelin'?" The question came from Grady Leathers, who had paused in the doorway, posing as if for a photo op.

"It'll be a few days before I'm ready to square dance again," Conrad replied as Leathers approached the bed.

"What happened?"

"Couple of our esteemed citizens used him as a football," the sheriff said. "Appears they don't like Jewish folks, which he says he isn't."

Leathers' ears and cheeks flushed until he reminded Conrad of a red cabbage wearing a gray mustache. "Conrad, please accept my apologies for this." He turned to the sheriff. "I won't have that kind of behavior in my district. Do you get my meanin', Sheriff?"

Now the cabbage syndrome spread to Rogers. "Yessir, I understand. But with all due respect, I don't need you bleedin' indignation all over me. I know my job, and I'll do it."

"Where are you gonna start?" Leathers said, taking a step closer to Rogers.

Not giving ground, Rogers said, "There's not a lot to go on."

"In other words, you should have left after you said, you understand."

"I'm not gonna stay here and trade barbs with you, Congressman. I've got work to do." He turned to Conrad. "Mr. Green, I'll be in touch."

Leathers watched Rogers leave, then looked at Conrad. "I'm ashamed for what happened to you. And I'm not gonna put up with it. So you're *not* Jewish?"

"No. My name and my ancestors came from England."

"But your assailants thought otherwise."

"Sounded that way to me."

"Good."

In response to the questioning look on Conrad's face, Leathers explained. "Of course this whole episode stinks. I said 'good' because the Jewish angle will allow us to classify this as a hate crime. So there's an excellent chance I can get the district office of the FBI involved in the investigation. And I certainly intend to explore that possibility. How badly are you hurt?"

"Aside from this pizza on the side of my head, I've got a couple of cracked ribs. But they say I can probably go home later today."

"I'm glad it wasn't any worse. From here on, you need to be careful. The ones who did this may not believe your people are English. Nothin's more dangerous than a southern boy who gets it into his head that he needs to teach somebody a lesson. Now I gotta go. You take care of yourself."

Leathers turned and looked at Ann Neville, who had been sitting quietly nearby. "Pardon me for not speakin', Miss Ann. But I did see you over there. He can use a good friend just now and I know he's in good hands with you."

Leathers left without looking back. When he was out of hearing range, Ann got up and walked to the bedside. "Is there a chance you *will* move?"

Lowering his voice, Conrad said, "Long term, I really don't know. But I can't leave now… I *won't* leave. We still have work to do… unless you'd rather not be around me now."

"Don't be foolish. We started this together, and we'll finish the same way."

"Look… this Jewish thing… It's possible… even likely, that was just a cover to hide the real reason I was attacked."

Ann saw his point immediately. "Ohhh, you think someone is worried about the questions we've been asking."

"If they're so disturbed that they'd put me here, they might be willing to do the same to you."

Ann thought a moment, then said, "I don't believe in my entire life I've ever taken a personal risk to stand up for something that needed a champion. I've done it by contributing money, and sometimes time, but neither of those is real commitment, not the kind you're willing to give. This may be my last chance to find out who I really am. I can't turn my back on that."

"You sure?"

"Yes."

"Okay. If they let me out of here later today, we'll go see Doc Marshall tomorrow morning… that is if you can find out where he lives."

"I'll get right on it. Earlier you mentioned that the barber might know."

"That's where I'd start."

16

"I'VE GOT FIVE after ten," Conrad said, looking at his watch. "Do you agree?"

Ann reset her watch, then said, "Agreed."

They were sitting in Ann's car on the shoulder of a two-lane road out in the country. On the opposite side of the road was a dirt driveway that ran down a hill and disappeared into kudzu-covered trees. The name on the mailbox by the driveway was H. Marshall.

Conrad took out his cell phone. "If I'm not back in fifteen minutes, call the sheriff." He navigated to the sheriff's number, which he'd already put in his contact list, then handed her the phone. "If you need to make the call, just tap the number with your finger. Be sure to touch right over the digits."

As he got out of the car, Ann said, "I'd have my own cell phone, except I really don't need one... at least I didn't until today."

This wasn't the time to tell her all the ways her life would be easier with one, so Conrad simply said, "We'll manage."

"You know, this is not a great plan," Ann said. "If anything happens to you, all I'll be doing is calling for help that may arrive too late."

"I've got my .38. If you hear a gunshot, that would be another time to call the sheriff."

"You sure about this?"

"Can't think of any other way. See you in a few minutes."

Conrad crossed the road and started down the Marshall driveway, the impact of his shoes on the Mississippi dirt powering little dust balls into the air and coaxing small jolts of pain from his heavily taped ribs. The driveway descended so sharply that in less than a minute, when he glanced behind him he could no longer see the car.

Everywhere he looked, the ground flanking the driveway was covered with kudzu. It even cloaked the occasional tree that lifted the ubiquitous green canopy like a pole on a circus tent. The only sounds were the plop of his feet on the powdery soil and the hum of a dragonfly that seemed fascinated with his hair.

Two more minutes into his trek brought him to a small thicket of kudzu- decorated trees. Entering the grove, he found it a place of surreal beauty.

Emerging from the thicket moments later, he saw off to his right a small lake with kudzu growing right up to the bank on all sides. About forty yards away from where he stood, perched on a little hill overlooking the lake, was a small frame house with a porch facing the water.

He'd come out here with no idea if he'd even find Doc Marshall at home. But somebody was, because he saw a car parked next to the house.

⸙

BACK IN THE CAR, the screen on Conrad's phone went dark, and Ann had no idea how to bring back the sheriff's number.

⸙

HEART FEELING LIKE it was sitting just under his chin, Conrad stepped onto Marshall's porch and walked to the front door. He was thinking he should knock three times. Anything less was odd, anything more would be pushy.

Before he could even rap once, the door was yanked open by a large man with sad eyes deeply set in a drooping wrinkled face. The muzzle of the rifle pointed at Conrad's chest looked like a huge letter O as in, 'Oh shit.'

"How come you're on foot?" the old man said.

Startled by his sudden appearance at the door and also by the unexpected question, Conrad said, "I didn't want to impose by driving onto your property."

"So bein' it's just you makes a difference in your mind."

Still at a big disadvantage in the conversation Conrad said, "I see what you mean. Are you Doctor Marshall?"

"I am Henry Marshall, but I'm not a doctor. So, if you need help with that contusion on the side of your head, you're out of luck. Besides, it looks like it's already startin' to heal."

"I'm not here for that. I hoped we could talk about the disappearance of Felder Cameron."

Already as pale as diluted nonfat milk, Marshall's complexion faded. "That was a long time ago. I don't have anything to say about it. Now if you'll excuse me."

Still holding the rifle level, he stepped back and began to shut the door with his foot.

"That's not what Penn Rogers said."

Marshall lowered the rifle and came forward. "Rogers spoke about me?"

"Just two days ago."

The old man stepped out onto the porch, and Conrad backed up to give him room. "What did he say?"

"He implied that you and he shared some secret about the boy's disappearance."

"Can't imagine what he meant. Who *are* you? What's your interest in this?"

"I'm representing someone who wants to know what happened."

"You a lawyer... a detective?"

"I guess the latter comes closest to describing me. Why did you give up medicine?"

Marshall stared hard at Conrad, then, rifle barrel dangling at his side, he walked to the porch railing, where he looked out over the lake. Still facing the water, he began to talk. "After her son disappeared, his mother, Beryl, became deeply depressed. I thought that was all there was to it. I had no idea she was really ill."

He turned and leaned lightly against the railing, his eyes looking at the porch floor. "I was young and believed I knew it all, had no appreciation for how the mind can affect the body. I gave her sedatives and antidepressants, but she just grew weaker and weaker. Should have referred her to another doctor, but I was too stubborn. I wanted her to come to grips with what happened, to face reality. And then... she died."

He looked up, pain clouding his eyes. "I was the town's only doctor. Everyone trusted me, had faith in me. And I failed her. How could I continue in practice after that? How could I do *anything?*

"My wife couldn't understand why I became so withdrawn and miserable, so she left me. I don't blame her. Why *should* she stay? I had nothing to offer her. Practice in a small town doesn't pay much, so there wasn't a lot to divide. I'd inherited a modest annuity from my parents, which became significantly smaller after the divorce, but it was still enough for one person. Moved out here, and I've been here ever since."

He gestured to the land. "It's quiet, and I have my books to keep me company. As the years have passed, I think less and less about Beryl Cameron. And that's a blessing, don't you think?"

"Yes sir, I suppose it is."

Marshall's gaze returned to the porch floor, and he continued talking. "If only the boy hadn't disappeared... so much sorrow... so many lives affected. Beryl... then her husband, killed in that ferry accident in Indonesia. Wouldn't have been there if he hadn't been trying to escape the horror of what happened here.

"And their poor daughter. With both parents gone, having to spend the rest of her life at Oakmont. I should visit her there. Yes... I should do that. Visit her..."

Marshall now seemed to be talking to himself. Not wanting to intrude on the old man's thoughts, Conrad turned and headed quietly back to where Ann waited.

17

"BOY, AM I GLAD to see you," Ann said as Conrad got back in the car. She held out his phone. "The screen on this thing went dark shortly after you left, and I didn't know what to do."

Conrad cringed. "Sorry, I forgot about that. If we ever get in the same situation again, you hit this button once, then when it lights up, press it again. And see... the number's back."

"Let's not *get* in this situation again. Did you talk to him?"

He recounted his meeting with Marshall.

"What a sad story," Ann said, when he finished. "Do you believe him?"

"He was very convincing. But if he's telling the truth, why'd Rogers say what he did?"

"You told me earlier that Rogers was confused when you spoke. Maybe what you heard was all something in a delirium."

"He didn't seem feverish at the time."

"Mercy, this is a difficult puzzle."

"Why isn't Beryl giving us more help?" He looked up and made a pleading gesture. "Beryl... we need you."

"Maybe she's not helping because she doesn't know any more than we do."

"I suppose that *could* be it. Hell, I have no idea how any of this works."

They sat for a moment thinking, then Ann said, "That daughter Marshall mentioned. It sounds like she's still alive. And Oakmont is only ten miles from here. Let's go talk to her."

"Isn't Oakmont a home for the autistic?"

"I know, but there are different levels of that affliction. If she can communicate, maybe she could tell us some little thing that would help."

Conrad shrugged. "Worth a try."

⁓

RONI ELLISON, STAFF supervisor at Oakmont was an attractive redhead, perfect complexion, eyes sparkling with intelligence, a trim figure shown to good advantage in her tailored business suit. She had personally escorted Ann and Conrad into her office.

"So that was *you* I saw across the street last week moving into the Rutledge house," Ann said. "Welcome to the neighborhood."

"Thank you," Ellison said. "I just love it there. Your azaleas are gorgeous."

"I can't take any credit for that. They just seem to thrive without any care."

Ellison turned to Conrad. "I don't want to embarrass you, but I think you're one of the finest writers of our time."

"You obviously have exquisite taste in literature," Conrad said pleasantly, without any hint of flirtation in his manner.

Ann found Conrad's apparent immunity to Ellison's beauty endearing and worrisome at the same time. His unwavering dedication to his late wife's memory was a noble thing, but some day he would have to find a way to move beyond his grief. And she wasn't sure he would ever be able to do that.

Ellison let her eyes linger on Conrad a bit longer than necessary, then said, "So... you're both interested in Janine Cameron."

"We're researching the events surrounding her brother's disappearance years ago and thought if we knew more about her, it might give us a better understanding of what happened," Conrad said.

Giving him a million-watt smile, Ellison said, "For a future book?"

"Too soon to say."

"I'd be happy to tell you what I know. Please…" she gestured to the two chairs in front of her desk. "Have a seat."

Ellison returned to her own chair and folded her hands on the desktop. "Janine arrived long before I did and is now our senior client-in-residence. According to her file, she was twelve when she came to us. The work-up done at the time of her admittance indicates that before the age of twelve, she showed unmistakable signs of autism, but it was relatively mild. She could dress herself and communicate effectively with other members of the family. There was hope she might one day be able to function at some minimal level in society. But then, the disappearance of her brother seemed to send her deeper into her affliction."

Ellison leaned back in her chair and dropped her hands into her lap. "She remained able to dress and feed herself and care for her personal hygiene, but stopped talking entirely. I don't believe she's said another word to this day, at least not where anyone here has heard it. And she sleeps only a half hour or so each night, usually just before dawn, spending most of the night sitting up in bed, staring into space."

Ellison shook her head. "I just don't know how a person can do that for fifty years. Her mother died the same year her brother went missing, and the next year her father drowned in a boating accident somewhere in Asia. Without her parents there was no one to care for her, so she was sent here. Fortunately, her father left her an annuity that pays for everything."

"There's no way at all to communicate with her?" Conrad said.

"Sometimes from her eye movements, we think she hears and understands what's said to her, but there's never any overt response. She's neat and no trouble at all, unless of course, she runs out of watercolor supplies."

"So, she paints," Ann said.

"Constantly."

Ann said, "That seems healthy."

"You would think so, but she always paints the same thing." Ellison got out of her chair and went to a nearby watercolor hanging on the wall. "This is hers."

Ann and Conrad went over to the painting to get a better look.

The work was rough and impressionistic, appearing to depict a landscape with woods in the background and a field in front.

"These look like people," Conrad said, pointing to a pair of pink objects in the center of the painting. He shifted his finger to a dark object off to the side. "But what's this?"

"We're not sure. Members of the staff have variously identified it as a barrel, an old stove, or a dozen other things."

"Is it a real location or made up?" Ann asked.

"No one knows. But real or imagined, it's firmly ingrained in her. Beginning about six months after she arrived, she's painted it every day for the last fifty odd years. Would you like to see her?"

"I don't think so," Ann said. "She can't talk, so there's really no point."

Ellison said, "She never has visitors. It might make her happy."

"No visitors?" Conrad said. "That's awful. Ann, I think we should see her."

Ann nodded. "All right."

They left Ellison's office, went down a carpeted hall and through a pair of institutional double doors, into a wing with a tiled hallway and neutral beige walls decorated with huge photos of various kinds of butterflies. At the first doorway on the right, Ellison paused and knocked on the open door. "Janine, you have visitors."

Ellison led them into a small room equipped with a bed, nightstand, dresser, and a leather club chair with a floor lamp beside it. On the walls were many duplicates of the painting in Ellison's office.

Janine was standing on the far side of a large wooden table using a wide brush to make broad confident strokes on a piece of watercolor paper. She was a little overweight and had long, straight, blonde hair mixed with gray. Her face was expressionless and unlined so she looked younger than her age. She gave no indication she even knew anyone else was in the room.

"Janine, this is Ann Neville and Conrad Green. Ann lives in your house in Glenwood Springs and Conrad lives next door. They heard about you and wanted to meet you."

Janine stopped work and looked at Ann. She picked up the painting she was working on, came around the table, and laid it out again so everyone could see it. As expected, it looked just like all her other paintings.

Janine looked again at Ann, then began jabbing at the painting with her finger, cycling between the pink figures in the center and the dark object off to the side.

"Yes, dear," Ann said. "It's very nice."

Unaffected by the compliment, Janine kept up that same behavior.

Having no idea what she should do next, Ann glanced at Ellison for help.

Ellison stepped closer to Janine and touched her gently on the shoulder. "It's a fine painting, dear. One of the very best you've done. But it's not complete. Wouldn't you like to finish it now?"

Janine ignored Ellison and became more agitated, her eyes alternating between Ann and the painting, her finger now hitting the paper hard, smudging the work.

"I think we'd better go," Ellison said, herding Ann and Conrad toward the door.

Conrad was afraid Janine would follow them, but she remained at the table finger-stabbing the painting.

When they were once more on the other side of the double doors, Ellison said to Ann, "That was extraordinary. I've never seen her respond to someone like she did to you."

"What was she trying to say?"

"I have no idea."

18

"WHY DO YOU THINK Janine behaved like that toward me?" Ann asked, sitting in Conrad's car immediately after leaving Oakmont.

"Considering how oddly her brain is wired, it could be a mistake to look for meaning in anything she does," Conrad replied.

"I'm not so sure. In any event, tonight, I won't sleep very well myself thinking of how long she's been there and how if her brother hadn't disappeared, she might have had a much better life. What's your impression of Ellison?"

"Nice woman."

"Attractive?"

"I suppose."

"I believe she thought the same about you."

"More likely she was wondering how I got this bruise."

"Doubt it."

IT WAS NOW a little before six o'clock. Needing time to figure out what to do next, Conrad and Ann had gone to their respective homes, planning to stay there until one of them had a decent idea about how to proceed.

At the moment, Conrad was standing in front of Claire's photo in his study.

Then the doorbell rang.

Who the devil would come to his house without calling first, he thought, forgetting that he'd done the same thing to Doc Marshall that very morning. He grabbed his .38 off the desk, hurried downstairs, and looked through the peephole in the front door.

Satisfied with what he saw, he shoved the gun into a pocket of the cargo pants he still wore from his visit to Doc Marshall, and opened the door.

There on the porch, stood Roni Ellison, a piece of rolled-up art paper in one hand.

"I'm so sorry to bother you," she said. "But after you left, Janine painted something a little different than anything she's done before. After the way she acted when you and your friend were there earlier, I thought you should see it… that maybe you'd find it significant in some way."

Not even considering that Ann would have been the more logical person to bring the painting to, Conrad said, "Please come in."

While Conrad closed the door behind her, Ellison took a quick look around, then turned to face Conrad as he moved away from the entrance.

"Is that it?" Conrad said, gesturing to the rolled-up paper.

"Yes."

Ellison held the painting out to him. As he reached for it, she shivered a little and her arm jerked upward, causing their hands to touch. Conrad pulled his hand back as though shocked by a jolt of static electricity.

"Sorry," Ellison said. "There's a cold front and some rain coming. Guess I got a little chilled." She again offered him the painting.

He took it without incident and unrolled it. "This one has a window frame around it," he said. "That sort of suggests it's something she really saw. Of course, I'm only guessing."

"I don't want to keep you," Ellison said. "Just came by to drop that off. You can hold onto it, if you like."

She turned toward the door, and Conrad opened it for her. "Thanks for coming. If you need an extra hand moving anything, let me know."

Giving him a lingering smile, Ellison said, "I'll do that."

After she was gone, Conrad got out his phone and called Ann.

No answer.

That worried him.

Of course, she could simply not be home. Just to be sure, he left his house, took a cautious look around, then walked down to where he could see her driveway.

No car.

Hoping she was simply running an errand, he returned home.

Over the next two hours, he called her three times, each unanswered ring increasing his concern for her safety. On the last call, he left a message describing Janine's new painting and asking her to call him as soon as she got in. He really did need to talk to her about getting a cell phone.

Shortly after he left the message about the new painting, Ann called back.

No... Not Ann. Caller origin showed *unknown name*.

"Conrad Green."

"Mr. Green, I have a story of interest to tell you," a muffled voice said. "Go to the pay phone at the Circle K next to the Great Wall restaurant and wait for my call."

"Who is this?"

"I don't want to say."

"How do I know you aren't one of the thugs who beat me up trying to get at me again?"

"You don't. But sometimes gain requires risk. I'll call you again at the Circle K phone in ten minutes. If you're not there, I'll assume you're not interested in finding the Cameron boy."

The caller hung up.

Conrad paced the floor, trying to decide what to do. Should he go or not? He paced some more. *Go or stay?*

Noting through the bedroom window that it was now raining heavily, he stopped at the downstairs closet and got a raincoat before leaving the house.

꽃

HUDDLED IN HIS RAINCOAT, its hood over his head, Conrad stood by the pay phone waiting for the promised call, well aware that he could be risking another attack. The mystery caller was probably watching to see if he'd brought the sheriff along. Why else would they have set up this cloak-and-dagger operation? A shiver started in the small of his back and crawled up to his neck. And it wasn't because of the weather. The guy had said ten minutes. He checked his watch… twelve minutes had passed since he'd left home. *This was nuts. Standing out here like a beer bottle sitting on a fence, waiting to be shot. To hell with this.*

As he turned to get back in his car, the pay phone rang.

Conrad stepped over and grabbed the receiver. "This is Green."

"Leave the parking lot, go up to the Shell station, drive around the convenience store, then come back here to the phone and wait five minutes."

"Is all this really necessary?" Conrad said, letting his irritation show.

"Yes."

"Maybe I'll just go home."

"Up to you. If you're not there when I call back, consider it opportunity lost."

Conrad hung up and jumped back in his car. Now he was sure of it. Whoever this was wanted to be certain no uninvited guests would be coming to the party. Actually, if this guy was legit, they both wanted that. Okay, so he'd play along. And he'd be watching too, for anyone following him.

꽃

CONRAD WAS WAITING by the phone when it rang again.

"Green."

"Go to the Sherwood Elementary School and drive around to the back parking lot," the same voice as before said. "Do you know where the school is?"

"Yes."

"It's a seven-minute drive from where you are, but I'll wait fifteen, no longer."

⸺❖⸺

THE RAIN WAS BEATING down so hard, Conrad's windshield wipers could barely keep up with it. The schoolyard had no lights whatever. Between the gloom and the rain, he could see only what was immediately in front of him. Realizing once again how dumb it was to be there, he reached over and picked up his .38 from the passenger seat.

The drive he was on was flanked by two tall brick buildings, so it didn't seem likely he was in any danger at the moment, but … The building on the left gave way to open space. Now he grew even edgier.

Then the building on the right ended. Ahead, two dumpsters forced him to turn right. There, in his headlights was a waiting car, sitting perpendicular to his, a small amount of blue smoke issuing from its exhaust, its lights also on.

The passenger door of the other car flew open. A hooded figure in a raincoat slid out and came rapidly toward the passenger side of Conrad's car. Whoever it was didn't seem to be carrying anything. Still, Conrad's heart was banging in his ears.

The figure reached the passenger door and tried to open it. Finding it locked, he motioned for Conrad to let him in. For a moment Conrad just sat there, weighing the situation. *If this had been a trap and the guy intended to shoot him, wouldn't he have come to the driver's side and motioned for the window to be rolled down? Or just start blasting away through that window?*

Yeah, the fact he was on the other side was a good sign… wasn't it?

The guy again motioned to be let in.

Conrad cocked the .38, muttered, "Oh crap," and unlocked the door.

19

THE GUY IN THE raincoat opened the car door, slid into the passenger seat, and shut the door. He stroked the hood of the raincoat off his head.

Conrad was shocked.

It was the handyman, Nate Goodrich.

"Nate. I had no idea that was you on the phone."

"Wasn't me. It was my son, Grif. He's over there drivin' that car."

"What do you want to tell me? And why are you being so secretive?"

"I know what went on with the Cameron boy. I have since the day it happened."

Suddenly, from behind, the area was flooded with lights from another vehicle entering the lot. The uninvited car sped past, jerked to a stop, and aimed a spotlight at Conrad's car. Despite the bright light in his eyes, Conrad saw two men wearing panty-hose masks and carrying baseball bats get out and split up, one heading for him, the other for Nate.

Conrad punched the button to lock Nate's door. An instant later, that window exploded, covering Nate in broken glass. As Conrad took a shocked breath, the glass in his window also shattered.

The thug on Nate's side rocked back and drove the fat end of the bat toward Nate's head. But Nate ducked, and the bat missed. On Conrad's side, that guy tried the same thing while saying, "I don't see no For Sale sign in your yard." The sudden movement necessary to avoid getting clobbered in the face cost Conrad an agonizing jolt of pain from his damaged ribs.

"I'm armed, you bastard," Conrad said, raising the .38. "So you better…"

And thus, Conrad made the mistake most ordinary people commit when confronting someone who lives on the fringes of humanity. Instead of just firing, he gave him a warning.

Quick as a bird's thought, Conrad's attacker lunged and hit the gun with the end of the bat. At the same time, he ducked to his left, so the windshield support would give him some shielding if the gun went off, which it did, just before it fell out of Conrad's hand and rattled onto the floorboard. The slug hit nothing as it went out the broken window, but the sound of the blast in the confined space of the car nearly broke Conrad's eardrums.

The guy lunged again with the bat, this time grazing Conrad's chin. Nate had grabbed the end of the other assailant's bat and was now being shaken like a dog toy.

Out of the corner of his eye, Conrad saw Nate's son get out of his car. He was enormous, at least six foot eight and weighing maybe three hundred pounds. And he was fast. In an instant, he was within grabbing distance of the man attacking his father. That guy pulled his bat out of Nate's hands and made a Babe Ruth cut at Grif, who, with one hand, caught the bat in mid-swing. Grif yanked the bat away from the thug and threw it on the pavement.

Conrad was able to see all this because the one attacking him had rushed toward Grif. This left Conrad free to look for his gun, which he did with one searching hand while keeping his eyes on the action.

Conrad's assailant took a bat swing at Grif, achieving the same result as his buddy, except this time, Grif flipped the bat around in his hand and got ready to do some batting practice himself.

Obviously realizing they were very much overmatched, the two hoodlums ran for their car and piled in. The driver made a tight reverse turn and they left the way they'd come, but this time with tires squealing. Suspending the search for his gun, Conrad straightened in his seat and put his foot on the brake pedal, hoping to get enough illumination from his brake lights to see the thugs' license plate in the rearview mirror. But the number seemed to be covered in burlap or something similar.

"You okay, Daddy?" Grif said to his father through the broken window.

"I am. But next time, try to get out of the car a little sooner. What were you doin'?"

"Listenin' to a lecture on DNA repair."

Nate looked at Conrad, who had just retrieved his gun from the floorboard. "He's been admitted to Ole Miss med school. Starts next fall."

"Good for you, Grif. And thanks for helping us. We'd have been in big trouble without you."

"My pleasure, Mr. Green."

The rain had let up a bit, but was still coming in through the car's broken windows.

"Nate, I'm sorry about this," Conrad said. "I had no idea I was being tailed. Those guys put me in the hospital yesterday. I didn't want to drag you into it."

"We went to a lot of trouble to make sure you *weren't* bein' followed," Nate said. "And obviously did a poor job of it, so we have to take a good share of the blame. I didn't want them to see me. But what's done is done. Now we ought to put this place behind us. We'll follow you home and you can get your car out of the rain. Then come sit with me and we'll talk."

With two windows gone, it was a wet, windy ride home. But Conrad barely noticed because he was focusing so much on what Nate was about to tell him. Reaching his driveway, he pulled under the side portico, got out, and climbed into the backseat of the Goodrich car, where Nate was waiting.

"Nate, back there at the school, you said you didn't want those thugs to see you. That sounds like you know something about them."

"Part of what I have to tell you will explain. But let me start at the beginnin'." He looked at his son, sitting behind the wheel.

"Grif, you don't want to hear any of this. Go wait in Mr. Conrad's car."

Grif nodded and obeyed, taking a big load off the vehicle's springs.

"I know what happened to Felder Cameron because I was there," Nate said as Grif dropped his massive bulk into the backseat of Conrad's car. "Saw it all. They weren't in Piney Woods like Leathers said. They were in Bailey Acres, behind your house. I was back there too, catchin' grasshoppers to go fishin'. When I heard them comin,' I hid."

As Nate spoke, Conrad could see the scene unfold in his mind…

BAILEY ACRES—JUNE 8, 1960

Grady Leathers swung the long stick in his hand, neatly lopping the flower off one of the many Queen Ann's Lace plants bordering the narrow path. "That's ten," *he shouted to Felder Cameron, who was lagging behind.* "How many have you done?"

"I don't know," *Felder said, swinging his stick at a flower that was too far off the path to reach.* "Didn't realize we were counting."

"All of life is a competition. That's what my daddy says. The ones who don't know that get left behind. Maybe that's why you're back there and I'm up here."

"You're up there because you got longer legs and can walk faster."

"Hey, here's a snake," *Leathers said excitedly, leaving the path and poking at the ground with his stick.*

Felder picked up the pace and followed Leathers into the weeds, where, far from the path, Grady lost the snake, but found something else. "Look at this."

When Felder reached the spot, he saw Leathers staring at a round wooden lid sitting on a single ring of brick.

"Help me lift it," *Leathers said, already bending over to grab one side.*

Between the two of them, they got the heavy lid up and flipped it over into the weeds on the other side. They were now staring into a gaping black hole that seemed to be lined with bricks all the way down.

"It's a well," *Felder said.*

"Well, duh… anybody can see that. Find a stone. I want to know how deep it is."

They scoured around until Leathers found some broken bricks several feet away, initially hidden by weeds. He carried a piece back to the well and tossed it in. Several seconds later, they heard a splash.

"Boy, it's really far down," *Felder said.*

"Wonder if there are any fish in it," *Leathers replied.*

"How would they get there?"

"Maybe it connects with the river."

"That's not how wells work."

"But this one could."

Felder shook his head. "Don't think so."

"Why are you so sure you're right about everything?"

"I'm not. I just know about wells."

"No, you think you know about everything. Just because you get better grades than I do doesn't mean you're always right and I never am. I'll wrestle you for it. Winner is right."

"I don't want to. Besides, that doesn't make any sense."

"Why not. You afraid?"

"I just don't want to do it."

Leathers walked over to Felder and shoved him. "Chicken."

"Stop it. I am not chicken."

Leathers pushed Felder again, harder. "Big chicken."

Felder stumbled backward under the force of Leathers' shove. Then Leathers did it again even harder. "Chicken."

"Stop it."

His face growing red in resonance with his increasing hostility, Leathers charged Felder and put him in a headlock. Struggling to get away, Felder led Leathers in a spinning, staggering dance that ended with them falling to the ground, still locked together. The impact of their fall caused Leathers to loosen his grip, and Felder slipped free.

"What's *wrong* with you?" *Felder said, getting to his feet.*

Leathers sat up and smacked the ground with his hand. His glasses were now askew on his face. He took them off and examined them. "Now look what you did. My glasses don't fit right anymore."

"I didn't do it, *you* did."

Leathers got to his feet and reset the glasses on his face as best he could. "You have to tell my father it was your fault."

"No. You *made* me wrestle."

"You're responsible," Leathers said, raising his voice to a shout. "And you better tell him." He said those last words in a weird combination of screaming and blubbering, spit flying out of mouth.

Felder turned and set off toward the path. "I'm going home."

Enraged, Leathers ran after him and pushed him in the back with both hands sending Felder sprawling on his belly. From the weeds, Leathers grabbed a broken piece of brick and straddled the smaller boy. Raising the brick over his head, Leathers brought it down with all his strength onto Felder's head, driving his friend's cheek into the ground.

For a moment, Leathers stared at Felder's unmoving body, blood pouring from a gash in the boy's head. Then he said, "Felder, are you okay? I didn't mean it. You aren't chicken."

He bent down and spoke into Felder's ear. "Come on Felder, talk to me… I give up. There aren't any fish in the well. You were right."

Leathers put two fingers under Felder's nose. He kept them there for a few seconds, then grabbed the boy by the shoulder and shook him. "Wake up… You have to wake up."

Getting no response, Leathers stood and looked helplessly around him. He glanced back where their argument had started. Lips clenched, he grabbed Felder by the feet and pulled him through the weeds to the well. There, he rolled the body up onto the lining bricks, where it balanced precariously for a moment before another shove from Leathers sent it tumbling into the yawning opening. As Leathers leaned over to look down the well, his glasses slipped off and followed Felder's body.

Leathers moaned and kicked the upper row of bricks lining the well. Then he ran back and got the bloody brick, returned to the well, and tossed the brick into the darkness. Grunting with effort, he managed to get the lid back on the well before fluffing up all the trampled grass.

He brushed the dirt from his clothes, then headed for home, not once glancing back to where his friend was now entombed.

20

"WHAT DID YOU DO after Leathers left?" Conrad asked Nate.

"Went to the well, took off the cover, and called down to the boy. But I didn't get any answer. So I ran home to find my daddy. He and my uncle and I came back with a rope and a flashlight, and my daddy went down into the well. But it was too late. The bottom had enough water in it that he couldn't even see the body. There was nothin' we could do to help, so we went home."

"And in all the time since, you never told anyone else what happened?"

"You have to understand… in the South back then, black folks didn't mess in white folks' business, particularly those with money and position like the Leathers family. Believe me, it ain't been an easy burden to carry, 'specially seein' Grady Leathers makin' himself out to be such a saint."

"I see what you mean," Conrad said. "I really do. There's no statute of limitations on murder, so Leathers could still be prosecuted. In addition to eliminating any chances of reelection, he might serve time. Could be prosecuted as an adult, even though he committed the crime as a child. There is precedence for such cases."

"And those men who beat you up—he sent them."

"How do you know that?"

"My cousin works for him as a maid. She heard him arrange the attack on the phone. He was tryin' to get you to leave town so you'd stop askin' so many questions."

"Why come forward now?"

"You bein' hurt was what finally pushed me into it. I almost told you the day you found me workin' in the tree. The idea of the little boy's spirit just hangin' around tryin' to get to his mother... that was so awful, I wanted to make it right. But I was scared, so I put that article through your mail slot hopin' it'd point you in the right direction and you'd somehow figure it out with no more help. I was scared then, and I still am. We're talkin' a U.S. congressman here, and one that'll do anything to protect himself."

"You know, because you work for me from time to time, once you decided to tell me directly what happened to Felder, you could have just come to the house and done it. Nobody would have had any idea what we talked about. The pay phone calls and the elaborate instructions for us to meet weren't necessary."

"I was afraid you were bein' watched, and you *were*."

"Even so, how would they have known the content of a conversation that took place in my house?"

"If you suddenly got smarter about the whole thing right after I came over, they might have just gone after me and my family on a guess."

Conrad nodded. "Yeah... that was a risk *I* wouldn't take either." There was a brief pause in the conversation, an interval in which the only sound was the persistent rhythm of rain hitting the car's roof. Then Conrad said, "I'm wondering... was the town doctor involved in any way?"

"Not that I know of. Why?"

"The guy who was sheriff back then is in the hospital. When Ann and I visited him a few days ago and asked about Felder's disappearance, he got really defensive. So I went back alone late that night and sat in the dark pretending to be someone who knew everything. He was so confused, he bought it. From what he said, he clearly knew what happened, but had taken a bribe to keep quiet. He called me Doctor Marshall, so I naturally assumed..."

"I'll bet he thought you were Marshall Leathers, Grady's daddy."

"Why'd he call me Doctor?"

"Grady's daddy had a big cotton farm, but he made the money to buy that land from patents he held for cosmetic products. See, he had a Ph.D. in chemistry that he was real proud of, so everyone called him Doctor Marshall."

"Like you calling me Mr. Conrad."

"We do that sort of thing a lot around here."

"I remember the newspaper saying that the sheriff searched Bailey Acres. He must have figured out what happened and went directly to Marshall Leathers with it."

"What now?"

"Is the body still there do you think?"

"Don't know. I saw the well a few years later, and it had a concrete cap on it. I haven't been back since. Hard to say what's down there. Could be Grady or his daddy had the remains moved before the cap was put on."

"That'd be risky."

"So's leavin' 'em alone."

"We can't go out there on our own and look. It'll probably take a jackhammer to get that cap off, hardly something we can do without drawing attention to ourselves. And if we did find the boy, everything has to be documented by official sources."

"You want to go to the sheriff?"

"I think we have to."

"Are you forgettin' he's Penn Rogers' son? How's he gonna react when he finds out his daddy took a bribe to hide the facts? Or maybe he already knows. If he's in with Grady Leathers, it could go hard on us."

"I heard an exchange between them when they both visited me in the hospital after I was attacked. Didn't sound as though they like each other. Are you willing to go on the record in front of the sheriff with what you told me?"

Nate sat and stared for a moment at the rain beating on the windshield. "We mishandle this and we might disappear too."

"Suppose I can think of a way to protect ourselves."

"How?"

"We could write up everything we know and I'll send it to my lawyer in New York with instructions to open the envelope if anything happens to us."

"Why not just tell him to open it right away?"

"For now, I think we should control the flow of information. We don't want an outsider getting involved too soon."

Nate considered Conrad's proposal, then sighed. "All right."

"What about your cousin? Would she testify in court that she heard Leathers arrange for me to be attacked?"

"Can't say. Chances are, she won't."

"It'd be helpful if she would, but I don't think it's critical. Nate, you've done a good thing here."

Nate looked at Conrad and gave him a weak smile.

Before anything more could be said, Conrad's phone rang. It was Ann.

"Nate, I'm sorry. I have to take this call."

Nate nodded.

"Ann, I've been worried about you."

"Forgive me, I should have told you I was going to Memphis to visit my niece. That new painting of Janine's you mentioned in your phone message... We need to talk about it."

"I have to speak with you too. I'm here with Nate Goodrich. Some things have happened that we want to discuss with you. We'll be there in two minutes."

21

"SO THAT'S THE STORY," Conrad said, sitting in Ann's parlor with Nate. "Since you and I started this together, I wanted to tell you before we went to the sheriff."

Ann sat speechless for a moment, then said, "So *that's* what Janine was trying to tell us."

"What do you mean?"

"Before I left for Memphis I had occasion to go into a room upstairs I don't use, and I happened to look out a window that faces the field behind the house. It struck me that the view resembled the scene in Janine's paintings. But it was different enough that I didn't think any more about it. When I got home and heard your message that Janine's new painting had a window frame around it, I realized… Of course the view is different. It's been over fifty years. Trees have grown that weren't there then. She saw it all from her bedroom window, and she's been painting the scene ever since, trying to get someone to understand. The two pink objects in the paintings are her brother and Grady Leathers. The object no one could figure out is probably the well."

"Who's Janine?" Nate asked.

"Felder Cameron's sister," Conrad replied.

"Oh," Nate said. "I was thinkin' her name was Jane, but yeah, that's wrong."

"We visited her today at Oakmont, where she lives," Ann said. "She can't speak, but she paints over and over what she saw from her window that day."

"I had no idea anyone else was watchin'."

"Ann, you should understand... there'll be risk when we go public," Conrad said. He explained about the letter he was planning to send to his lawyer, then added, "Even so, you might want to distance yourself from us."

"I can't. I'm too firmly linked to the boy now. When you go see Rogers, I need to be standing right beside you. When will you do it?"

"I'll call tomorrow morning and try to get a meeting for ten o'clock. I'll let you both know if it's on or not."

-❦-

CONRAD ROSE EARLY the next morning to ease his mind on an issue that needed to be resolved before calling the sheriff. He threw on some clothes and grabbed Janine's newest painting, which he carried downstairs and out the back door. The tall stockade fence along his back property line didn't have a gate that would give him direct access to Bailey Acres. But Ann's yard was separated from Bailey only by a short picket fence he could easily step over. So he headed for the junipers between his yard and hers, then followed the trees back to Bailey, where he was disappointed to find no path through the waist-high weeds. *But then, why should there be one?*

No choice now but to plunge ahead.

It was commonly believed that the land back here consisted of forty acres. That was a lot of territory to explore if you were looking for something specific and had no idea where it might be. But Conrad had a map of sorts—Janine's painting.

He unrolled the watercolor, glanced at Ann's house, and then looked at what they believed was the well in the painting. With this as a general guide, he stepped into the weeds.

He was about ten yards in when he thought of two things that hadn't occurred to him until now: The field was probably full of ticks that carried who knows what. And he'd forgotten to bring his gun.

He quickly decided that none of that mattered, because there was no way he was turning back now.

As he fought his way deeper into the property, he kept an eye on the upper windows in Ann's home, trying to judge which way to go, fully aware that the perspective and relative distances on the painting might be entirely wrong.

His course took him past a tall hackberry tree that was not shown on the painting. Had Janine just ignored it, or was it not there at the time? No way to know.

A few steps later, he almost walked into a large web occupied by a huge spider with yellow stripes on a mottled black body. *Why would kids even want to come here?*

He next encountered a stand of tall plants exhibiting flat clusters of tiny flowers. It seemed like such a shame to trample them that he chose another route. His disturbance of the weeds and grasses as he moved caused tiny insects to fly up into his face and then head for quieter surroundings. Many of them didn't get far because they were picked off by two mockingbirds swooping in to take advantage of the walking buffet.

Another check of Ann's windows caused him to make a course correction to his right. This soon took him between two more hackberries that weren't on the painting. Another twenty yards through a stand of tall grass whose leaves felt like sandpaper, brought him to what looked like the general area where he should be.

Nearby was another hackberry that wasn't on the painting. This tree was so thick at the base it must have at least been a sapling when Janine had so firmly fixed the scene in her mind.

He was in the field because, despite his initial argument to go directly to the sheriff with Nate's story, he'd begun to feel that he shouldn't proceed without taking a look at the place where Felder Cameron's remains might still be. He didn't doubt anything Nate said, he just needed to see the well for himself.

To find it, he began tramping down the grass in an ever-widening circle, wishing now that he'd thought to bring a board with a rope on each end like those guys used to make crop circles in England. It took about two seconds to realize that just walking around like he was stamping grapes was going to take forever to cover any ground. So he adopted a modification of the technique he'd employed when searching for sawed-off fence posts at the Cameron family cemetery plot. He used one foot as an anchor and slid the other along the grass in as wide an arc as he could manage. By being careful, he could perform this maneuver while causing only minor complaints from his injured ribs.

In ten minutes he was exhausted. And the sun was now high enough that the vegetation he was wading through seemed to be radiating steam. Not prepared to give up, he was ready for a break, which he took sitting under the big hackberry. After three more cycles of searching, he still had not found the well. His failure showed him that he was right to have come out here. *Suppose the sheriff couldn't find it either?* Of course, *he* would most likely have brought help.

Help.

That's what was needed.

With that decision made, he followed the minimal path he'd created back through the weeds to where he'd first entered the field. Then, he pulled out his phone and called Nate. Being as diplomatic as he could about what he was up to, he managed to enlist Nate's assistance without offending him.

It would take Nate ten minutes to get there. Rather than just wait idly while he made the drive, Conrad headed for Ann's front door, which he reached in less than a minute.

He had no idea what her usual morning schedule was, but hoped sleeping late wasn't included. Apparently, he needn't have worried because she answered his ring fully dressed with every hair in place.

"Conrad... anything wrong?"

He explained what he'd been doing, then said, "Nate's on his way to help, but before he gets here, I thought we should look out the window where Janine was standing when the image she's been painting was burned into her mind. I tried to judge the right area from the ground looking back at your windows, but it might appear different from this direction."

She gestured at the rolled-up paper in his hand. "I guess that's the painting you told me about... with the window frame in it."

"Yeah, we could look out your window and have it right there with us for reference. Probably should have done that first."

"Come on."

Conrad followed Ann up her wide staircase to a long hallway carpeted with an antique Persian runner so plush their footsteps made practically no sound.

Suddenly, he felt the presence of Beryl Cameron accompanying them down the hall, as though she too, wanted to look out the window with them. Instead of making him shiver as such a phenomenon might have before the events of the past week, he was pleased that she seemed to know her long torment would soon be over.

If in fact, the progress he believed they were making, was real.

"It's in here," Ann said, stopping at a door halfway down the hall.

She led him into a room that most large homes have: a catchall space where unneeded things that were too good for the attic ended up. This one mostly contained framed prints and oil paintings stacked against the walls.

She flicked on the lights. "It's this window," she said, walking over to the middle member of a triptych of wavy glass panels surrounded by dark oak stiles and rails.

Conrad unrolled Janine's watercolor, and they compared the view out the window with what was on the paper.

"I believe this thing way in the distance is the town water tower," Ann said, pointing to a feathery object in the painting that certainly looked like it was standing on legs and which, to Conrad's mind, did resemble the tower visible from the window.

"And this," she pointed to an indistinct blur in front of the tower. "is that house over there on Adams... there's a tree covering most of it now, but its gable lines are similar. To me, that puts the well...," she looked again at the brown smudge on the painting then shifted her eyes toward the field, "…in the general area of that big tree."

"That's what I thought too," Conrad said, "but so far, I haven't found it. Good to know that my instincts from down there agree with the view up here. Uh oh, there's Nate."

Conrad pulled out his phone, called Nate, and told him he'd be with him in a minute.

"I'm coming too," Ann said. "I'll put on some jeans and meet you in the field."

⁕

"LET'S TAKE A BREAK," Conrad said.

He, Ann, and Nate had been tramping down weeds, three abreast, in ever-widening circles around the big hackberry for a half hour. And had found nothing.

Nate and Ann headed for the shade of the hackberry, but Conrad remained where they'd stopped. He looked back at Ann's house, then surveyed all the ground they'd covered. Shaking his head, he followed Nate and Ann.

"Don't know why we haven't found it," Nate said, fanning his face with his straw hat. "I'm sure this is the area where it was."

"Maybe somebody came in here years ago, knocked it all in, and filled it with dirt," Conrad suggested.

Nate's mouth dropped open.

Seeing his reaction, Ann said, "Nate…?"

"I should have thought of this earlier when we were talkin' in your car about how Leathers and his father might have had the boy's remains moved," Nate said. "A few years after I saw that the well had been capped, there was a rumor this whole field was gonna be developed for new houses. They put a gate in the chain link borderin' Adams and a few dump trucks came and went, then all activity stopped and everything went back to normal."

"Sounds like either nothing's here now to find, or the well's been so hidden, the sheriff will have every reason to ignore what we tell him," Conrad said.

"Does that mean we're beaten?" Ann asked.

Conrad kicked a clump of trampled grass. "Appears that way to me.

22

CONRAD WOKE TO the familiar sound of crying coming from the garden.

He's back.

Exhilarated at the boy's return, Conrad leapt from the bed and ran to the window, where he saw the boy standing at the fence exactly as he had been on each of the other occasions he'd appeared. Previously, he'd always kept his eyes on the irises as he wept, but this time, apparently sensing Conrad watching him, he suddenly stopped crying and released his hold on the fence. He looked up at Conrad's window, raised his left arm, and pointed toward Bailey Acres. Then he brought his right arm up and showed Conrad three raised fingers on that hand.

Abruptly, Conrad woke from his dream.

Rattled and unsure whether he was awake or asleep, he sat up in bed and pinched himself.

"Oww!"

Okay, so it hurt, which, he now realized meant nothing. Maybe he was dreaming he'd pinched himself and that it hurt. He *felt* awake. But when he saw the boy a moment ago he didn't realize he was asleep, so that didn't mean anything either.

How the hell do you prove you're awake?

He got up and went to the window.

No little boy.

Looking at the clock, he saw it was 3 a.m. Every other time he'd seen the boy in the garden it had been 1 a.m. That suggested he'd been dreaming earlier and was now awake.

He got dressed and sat at the window until dawn, wondering if the boy had, by intention, invaded his dreams, or if his own brain had simply created the event out of need.

The latter had occurred often in his writing life. When he'd hit a plot obstacle he'd tell his brain how important it was that an answer be found. And invariably, the problem would be solved while he slept. Was that what had just happened? The boy's hand extending toward Bailey Acres was a clear indication that the well was still there, and the three fingers was a clue to its exact location. If the riddle had come from *his* brain and not the boy, the subconscious Conrad already knew what the three fingers meant. But the conscious Conrad had no damn idea.

As soon as he saw the thin light of dawn begin to wash over the garden, he picked up his phone and called Ann.

"It's Conrad. I'm sorry to call you so early, but I think the well is still in the field, and I believe the boy's remains are in it. I need to look out that window of your house again. Can I come now?"

"What's happened?"

"It's complicated. I'll tell you when I see you. Should I walk slowly, so you have a chance to get dressed?"

"Just get here. I'll be ready."

And she was.

"Story please," she said, letting him in.

He related his dream and waited for her reaction.

"Do you know what the three fingers mean?"

"No. But I might if I look again."

"Then let's go."

Moments later when they reached the window, Ann hung back so Conrad would have an unobstructed view. If the next instant had taken place in a comic book, the panel would have had the word POW! emblazoned across a big white star because Conrad immediately saw the answer to the three-finger riddle.

HEART STILL THUDDING against his breastbone after he'd solved the riddle from his dream, Conrad stepped out of Ann's back door and stood for a moment. Too impatient to go all the way to the path he'd created the day before, he took a straight route to Ann's back property line, stepped over her little picket fence, and started a new path, Ann close behind.

Moving through the field from that point required minimal effort until they encountered a large patch of wild blackberries.

After a wide detour, they reached the perimeter of the previous day's search, where, already, the weeds were beginning to recover from their footsteps. Conrad had still not told Ann what he had discovered from her window, but he didn't have to. Given the three-finger clue, she'd seen for herself that the big hackberry where they'd sought shade the day before was not a single tree, but three individual trees that had grown together at their combined base.

Conrad reached the fused hackberries first and dropped to his knees. He searched a moment, then, with a trowel he'd borrowed from Ann, began scraping near the ground where an arch of wood with a small defect in its center was almost hidden by grass.

Ann heard the ring of metal as the trowel hit something hard.

Conrad looked at her, grinned, and said one word, "Brick."

23

FROM BEHIND HIS DESK, Sheriff Rogers looked first at Conrad, then Nate, and finally Ann, his face a grim mask. "You know how serious this is?"

From where he sat, Conrad said, "Yes sir, we do."

Rogers turned to Nate. "If what you say is true, you could be exposin' yourself to prosecution for obstruction of justice. You prepared for that?"

"If it's the price for doin' what's right, then I'll just have to take what comes."

"And you're willin' to sign a statement and testify in open court about what you saw?"

"Yes."

"We're not talkin' some nobody here. Congressman Leathers runs this county. What he wants, he gets."

"That should all be over once the truth is known," Conrad said.

Rogers looked down his nose at Conrad. "But is it the truth? If I go out to that tree and there's no well…"

"It's there," Conrad said.

"Even if we don't advertise it, everybody in town is gonna know what we're doin' out there. If you're wrong, I'm gonna look stupid."

"Why?" Conrad said. "You'll just be doing what you were elected to do— follow up on a reported crime."

"Don't tell me my duty. Can you guarantee he's there?"

Conrad almost said yes, but the strong possibility that the dream about the tree had been his own doing, kept him quiet. Then, like Rogers and Ann, he looked at Nate.

"No, sir, I can't say he's still there. All I can tell you is what I saw that day."

Rogers pointed at the picture of his father on the wall. "Years ago, I discussed this case with my daddy. He said he took a search party into Bailey Acres and combed it thoroughly. If what you say is true, there should have been trampled weeds and blood on the ground where the crime took place. Even if they somehow missed that, they couldn't have failed to find the well. I know my daddy. He would have dragged that well for the body."

Conrad tensed, knowing the moment they all feared was at hand.

Rogers pointed his finger at Nate. "If your account is true, how do you explain that?"

Saying nothing, Nate looked at the floor.

Rogers in turn stared at Conrad, then Ann. "Speak up," he said. "I can see you all got somethin' to say. Let's hear it."

Conrad said, "We believe your father—"

Rogers leaned forward and pressed himself against the desk as if trying to reach Conrad through it. "What about him?"

"We believe he conspired with Marshall Leathers, Grady's father, to keep anyone else from learning what we've just presented to you."

Rogers' face grew purple with rage. "Who the hell told you that?"

"I'm afraid your father did."

In a challenging tone, Rogers said, "When?"

"Three nights ago in the hospital. He was confused and thought I was Marshall Leathers. He complained to me about coercing him into hiding the truth." Conrad hoped Rogers wouldn't ask the next logical question.

"And did you do anything to help him *be* confused?"

So much for that hope. "Only after he opened the door to the idea."

"Keep talkin'."

"Ann and I went to see him earlier in the day. When I asked him about the Cameron boy, he went on a rant about how he was a good sheriff and never took money from anybody. Wanted to know who said he did. That got me wondering… So I went back later that night, sat in the dark by his bed, and pretended to be whoever it was he'd conspired with. He called me Doctor Marshall and said I shouldn't worry because he didn't say anything to the people who earlier that day asked him about the Cameron boy. And he said he never would."

"Well… ain't you the clever big city detective, invadin' folks' privacy with no worries about it at all." He turned and studied the pictures on the wall of his father and himself, then looked back at Conrad. "Who else knows about this?"

"No one at the moment, but my lawyer in New York has a sealed letter detailing everything we've learned. Anything happens to us, he'll open it."

"Sounds like you're afraid of *me*."

"Just taking precautions."

"All right. I'll take a look."

"Is it okay if we're present?"

"Oh, I definitely want you all there. Should be able to do it some time tomorrow."

❦

ANN NEVILLE HURRIED into the kitchen and picked up the phone. It was now late afternoon of the same day they'd told the sheriff all they knew.

"Ann, this is Conrad. Meet me at the end of Bog Road in fifteen minutes. It's important. Know where that is?"

"Yes, but—"

He hung up.

24

ANN PULLED UP TO Conrad's car, which was behind Nate's truck. She got out and walked toward the two vehicles. As she approached the car, an unshaven creature in jeans and a long-sleeved work shirt popped out from in front of the truck. He was holding a handgun.

"C'mon, lady, we're goin' down the path over there."

Ann wasn't stupid. With all she and Conrad had discovered, she knew she was in serious, probably even lethal trouble. And she was powerless to do anything to save herself. So, like most people who find themselves in such a spot, she chose to obey the guy's order, hoping, unrealistically, that the situation wasn't as grim as it appeared.

She soon learned that the path he'd referred to was a steep one that quickly took the two of them below road level. The route was flanked by scrubby vegetation that blocked her view on either side. Nor could she see where the path led, because a few yards ahead it made a right angle.

Navigating that turn a moment later, she saw Conrad and Nate at the bog's edge, on their knees, wrists and ankles bound with duct tape. Sheriff Rogers was standing over them with a gun that looked every bit as big and ugly as the one at her back.

The thug with Ann herded her over beside Conrad then put a hand on her shoulder and pushed her down. "On your knees."

As she hit the dirt, Conrad turned to her. "Ann, I'm so sorry. They called you on my phone, but it wasn't me talking. There was nothing I could do to warn you."

143

"It didn't even sound like you," Ann replied. "I should have realized the truth."

"It's all my fault," Nate said. "They threatened to kill my family if I didn't call Mr. Conrad out here."

The guy who'd brought Ann down the hill headed back to the road apparently to act as a lookout.

Rogers came from behind them and stood off to the side, slightly in front of Nate, but far enough away that Nate couldn't lunge at him, not that the old handyman could have accomplished anything, bound as he was.

"Did you all really think I was gonna let you destroy my daddy's reputation?" Rogers said. "We stand for somethin' in this town. People respect us."

Nate dropped his head and began to mutter a prayer, but it didn't sound like he was speaking English.

⁂

AT THAT EXACT MOMENT, Daddy Rain was sitting on his porch, his head bowed like Nate's. Had anyone been around to hear, they would have wondered what the devil the old man was doing, because he too, was mumbling. And it wasn't in English either.

⁂

BACK AT THE BOG, Rogers continued haranguing his captives. "This was none of your business. You shoulda stayed out of it."

"I can't believe you're willing to kill three people just to protect a reputation," Conrad said. "That's lunacy."

"Wouldn't expect a Yankee to understand. You people don't respect anything."

"Aren't you forgetting the letter I sent my lawyer."

Rogers pulled an envelope from his back pocket. "This one? You shouldn't have mentioned it while I could still get to it."

Conrad was enraged at the whole situation. On top of his complicity in Claire's death, he had now failed Beryl and her son. Beryl would remain forever suspended in pain, separated from her boy. And Felder would wander through time, looking for his mother. Wasn't that enough responsibility for one man to bear? Apparently not, because in addition, Ann and Nate were about to die because he'd pulled them both into this. He'd put too much faith in that damn letter... come out here with his guard down... let Rogers and his lackey take his gun. A scream of fury rose in his throat, then flew from his lips, the sound carrying across the bog, frightening many of the birds that lived there.

Ann was already terrified at what was about to happen, but Conrad's roar of helplessness made her feel even worse. Nate though, was so immersed in prayer, he didn't seem to notice.

"Believe me," Rogers said. "I don't want to do this. But you forced me." He pointed the gun at Nate's head. Then something odd happened. Before Rogers could pull the trigger, blood began to trickle from one side of his nose. This was quickly followed by a similar discharge from his other nostril. He wiped at the flow with the back of his free hand, then stared at the blood on his skin in disbelief.

Conrad next saw blood begin to seep from the inner corners of Rogers' eyes, which were jittering in their sockets. So much blood was now coming from the man's nose, it ran into his gaping mouth.

Rogers' gun hand sagged and dropped to his side. Utterly confused and shocked, he looked down at the front of his pants, where a dark red Rorschach was spreading over the fabric. The gun slipped from his hand, and he staggered several steps to his left. Blood was now coming out of his ears, from beneath his fingernails, and in seconds, from under his shirt at his wrists. All the while, Nate kept muttering.

Without emitting a sound, Rogers collapsed onto the sand, still breathing, but not moving.

"Ann," Conrad shouted. "Get his gun before the other one comes back."

She grabbed the weapon, then, after a quick glance up the hill, managed to release Conrad's arms and legs. She handed him the gun and freed Nate, who had finally grown quiet.

Still no sign of the lookout.

Nate walked over to Rogers' prone body and gave it a nudge with his foot. "I think he's dead."

Conrad moved closer and trained the gun on Rogers' head. "Nate, be careful."

Not taking his eyes off the body, Nate said, "I'd check for a pulse, but I don't want to get blood on me."

"I can see the outline of a cell phone in his right pocket," Conrad said, "and there's no blood near it. Fish it out, and we'll call for help. Someone else can figure out if he's still alive."

When the phone was safely in Nate's hand and he'd moved away from the body, Conrad checked the hill for any sign of the lookout, but still didn't see him.

After Nate called 911, Conrad gestured to the body, "What the hell just happened here? What's wrong with him?"

Nate looked out over the bog. "I think Daddy Rain got him."

25

"THAT WAS THE ME, the medical examiner," Lieutenant Doug Lindsey of the Mississippi State Police said, hanging up the phone in Sheriff Rogers' office. Lindsey's skin was the color of strong tea, and he filled out his state trooper uniform like a linebacker. Everything about him was so starched and proper that even sitting on the edge of the desk he seemed to be standing at attention. It was now three hours after Rogers had bled out at the bog. Arrayed in chairs in front of the desk, Conrad, Ann, and Nate waited eagerly to hear the medical examiner's verdict of why that happened.

"It's preliminary," Lindsey said, "but it looks like the sheriff had an autoimmune disease that destroyed his platelets... those things in blood that keep us from bleedin' to death. ME never heard of a case where it came on so sudden and with such force, but that's probably what he's gonna put down as the cause of death. Lucky for you three, it hit him when it did." He slapped one thigh with the palm of his hand. "Guess we're through here. We'll be openin' that well tomorrow mornin' around ten. I'd like you all to be there."

❦

FIFTEEN MINUTES LATER, Conrad switched off his car's engine, and he and his two passengers got out and headed for Daddy Rain's porch where the old man was filling a hummingbird feeder.

"You hear what happened?" Nate said.

"I got wind of it," Daddy said, hanging the feeder on its hook.

"Mind if we sit?" Nate said.

When they were all seated, Conrad said to Daddy, "How is what you did possible?"

"What makes you think I did anything?"

"The sheriff... he was about to kill all of us, then blood just started running out of him."

"Sounds like he was sick to me," Daddy Rain said.

"The medical examiner said that too," Conrad replied. "But it peaked at a very convenient time. And just before it happened, Nate started mumbling something that sounded like a prayer, but he wasn't speaking English."

"Then Nate's the one to talk to."

"We discussed it and he has no idea what he was saying."

"Look," Daddy Rain said, pointing at the feeder. "It's an Anna, the only hummin' bird that produces a song."

"Then why isn't it singin'?" Nate said.

"Why aren't you?" Daddy Rain replied.

"Because I don't know why I did what I did."

"Neither does the bird."

Seeing that Daddy Rain wasn't going to talk about the sheriff bleeding to death, Conrad brought up something else he'd been thinking about... something worrisome. "Are we going to have any more trouble from the sheriff? I mean, those spirit doors that are open... Now that he's dead, can he come back through them?"

"The sheriff is in a much different place than either the boy or his mother," Daddy said. "The door to that one ain't ever comin' open."

※

THE SOUND OF A jackhammer was an incongruous intrusion on the normal serenity of Bailey Acres. The three-hackberry cocoon that enclosed the well had been opened by chainsaws, and the remains of those trees were piled off to the side. Now, a workman was trying to separate the concrete cover from the upper row of bricks lining the well. The trick was to do that without having a lot of debris fall into the hole.

The guy working the jackhammer shut it off, put it down, and whistled two other workmen over to give him a hand. Together, they raised the cap from the well and toppled it to the side, making sure it didn't hit the supports for the beam and pulley suspended over the well.

Even though the state police had men posted all around the perimeter of the field to keep out unwanted gawkers, there were still a lot of people there, including Conrad of course, along with Ann and Nate. The medical examiner was present too, a man so gaunt he was in no danger of getting dirt from his neck on the collar of his short-sleeved white shirt. He had brought along a tech in a white jumpsuit. This one's outfit looked simple enough that it could easily be put on over a regular set of clothes. Why he was already wearing it when he arrived was a puzzle, especially since they'd all been standing around for more than an hour. Probably didn't know how much had to be done before he'd be called on to do his job. Lieutenant Lindsey and two other state troopers rounded out the group.

The men who'd lifted the cap off the well fitted a sling seat and harness to the pulley system above the well, then the one apparently in charge gestured to the seat like a model showing off a new car. With a quick nod of acknowledgment to the ME, the tech in white reached into the blue bucket he'd brought, fished out a headlamp flashlight, and looped it over his head. He returned to the bucket for a pair of rubber gloves and demonstrated how quickly he could put them on.

Bucket in hand, the tech headed for the well, where the workmen soon had him lashed into the makeshift seat at the end of the pulley. Giving everyone a thumbs-up, the tech swung out over the well and quickly disappeared into it, his speed of descent controlled by a rope sliding through the hands of the biggest of the three workmen.

The ME dug a Handie-Talkie out of the leather satchel he'd brought and pressed the talk button. "How's it look down there?"

"Too soon to tell."

An air of expectancy hovered over the place. The possibility that they were all about to witness the end of a mystery that had festered for over half a century gripped the mind of everyone present. Even the dragonflies and bees working the field appeared to have settled somewhere to see what was about to happen, the pervasive silence broken only by the creak of the pulley as the lowering rope rolled over it.

Time dripped by slower than the liquid that had formed the stalactites in the culvert at Piney Woods. Finally, the ME's Handie-Talkie squawked again, "It's dry down here, and I think we've got something."

26

THE TECH'S WORDS from below caused everyone to move closer to the well. Conrad wondered what he meant... *we've got something*... bones... clothes... the brick Leathers used to kill the boy... *what?*

Suddenly, a loud voice from behind the group said, "Who's in charge here?"

Conrad knew even before turning around that the voice belonged to Grady Leathers.

"The State Police have taken control of this site," Lindsey said to Leathers. "I'm Lieutenant Lindsey. Who are you?"

"Grady Leathers, congressman for this district. I heard you may have found the Cameron boy." Behind Leathers, his toady, had a smug look on his face.

Earlier, when Conrad, Ann, and Nate had briefed Lindsey about the entire situation, the only detail they held back was the reason Conrad and Ann had initially begun their investigation. So the trooper knew that Nate had seen Leathers kill the boy. Like all good cops, neither Lindsey's expression nor the tone in his voice showed any emotion when he asked Leathers who had told him about the search underway.

Leathers, on the other hand, couldn't help letting his face and voice show his contempt at being questioned like a commoner. "I'm not free to say."

Even though Leathers had only been a kid when he'd killed Felder Cameron, Conrad felt like slugging him for the act and hiding it so long.

Further exchange between Lindsey and Leathers was interrupted by the crackle of the ME's Handie-Talkie. "Coming up…"

As the man on the rope began hauling the tech back to the light, everyone focused on his imminent arrival. Time now slowed even more. The thought that the boy and his mother's long separation might soon be over brought Conrad a sense of fulfillment deeper even than when his last book reached number two on the *Times'* list. In an odd way, the feeling was almost as if he was awaiting the birth of the child he and Claire had hoped for.

The top of the tech's head appeared, then he was all the way up. One of the workmen helped swing him toward solid ground, and the other helped him out of his harness.

Over the lip of the bucket, Conrad saw the rounded end of two large bones. Also seeing them, the ME put on a pair of rubber gloves from his satchel, then returned to it for a large blue towel that he spread on the ground. The tech sat the bucket at the ME's feet and stepped out of the way.

Looking at the tech, the ME said, "You get pictures down there before moving anything?"

The tech nodded, produced a cell phone from somewhere, and wiggled it triumphantly. Conrad was surprised that they would use such a common device to record something with so much potential legal significance.

The first object the ME took out of the bucket was a skull, which, from its size, obviously came from a child. When Lindsey had called the ME about the possible remains in the well, he hadn't mentioned how death might have occurred, which meant the ME didn't know that story. Even so, the skull occupied the ME's attention for several minutes as he turned it over and over in his hands.

Conrad was too far away to see any detail, but at one point, the ME tilted the skull, apparently trying to change the angle of the light striking the surface. Then he ran a finger over an area that he seemed to find of great interest. Finally, he put the skull on the blue towel and reached back in the bucket. This time he came out with the jawbone.

Over the next few minutes, the ME removed bone after bone from the bucket, examined each one, then placed it in its proper position on the towel, slowly reconstructing what turned out to be a complete, albeit small, skeleton. Had the sky not been full of large white clouds that often obstructed the blazing sun, watching him could have been uncomfortable, although Conrad was so invested in the proceedings, he probably wouldn't have noticed.

"So, what's the verdict, doc?" Leathers said, when the last bone had been placed.

Lindsey shot Leathers a fierce look, obviously intended to remind him which of them was in charge. The congressman lifted an apologetic hand and nodded in acknowledgment. But his face reddened at the rebuke.

Noting that exchange, the ME addressed his response to Lindsey. "The remains are from a male between the age of six and ten. If water was present in the well when the body was dumped, death could have been caused by drowning. Without the lungs that possibility must go unexplored. In any event, there's a depressed fracture on the right temporal bone that by itself could have been fatal."

"I also found this down there," the tech said, digging in his pocket. He pulled out a plastic bag and gave it to the ME. During the transfer, Conrad moved closer to see what was in the bag.

A small metal button.

Conrad's heart surged.

The ME examined the button without taking it from the bag, then handed it to Lindsey. "It's a bit rusty, but you can still see it has a New York Yankees' logo on it."

Earlier, Conrad and Ann had shown Felder Cameron's picture to Lindsey, so the trooper knew the button's significance. Lindsey held it up to the light, studied it briefly, then handed the bag to Conrad. "Looks like the same button to me."

Conrad examined it and showed it to Ann, who nodded.

"We think so too," Conrad said, returning the bag.

Speaking to the ME, Lindsey said, "We have a photo of the missing child wearing this button. And that skeleton is from a boy who was the right age. So there's no doubt in my mind it's him."

"Here's something else from down there," the tech said, stepping forward with another plastic bag. This one contained a pair of glasses.

The ME removed the glasses from the bag, examined them briefly, and rubbed at dirt on the inside of one temple. He held them out so Lindsey could see what he'd found.

Because he wasn't wearing gloves, Lindsey kept his hands to himself, and simply leaned in to inspect the temple. He then turned to Leathers. "Congressman, these glasses have your name inscribed on them. How do you suppose they got down in that well with those bones?"

Doing a good job of appearing puzzled, Leathers said, "I have no idea."

"Seems strange to me," Lindsey said. "At the time the boy disappeared, I understand you said you were both playin' in Piney Woods and you lost your glasses there lookin' for him. And here we find the boy's remains and your glasses in an entirely different place."

"It's bizarre," Leathers said.

"I agree," Lindsey replied. He looked at the two troopers standing nearby. "Gentlemen, take the congressman back to the sheriff's office and make him comfortable." He turned to Leathers. "You and I need to have a long chat. "I'll be along directly."

Leathers looked sharply at the toady he'd brought. "Tell my lawyer to book himself on a plane and get his ass down here immediately."

The two patrolmen, the toady, and Leathers, headed for the street, where the vehicles were parked.

Lindsey turned to the three workmen, who were standing around listening to everything that was said. "You all need to keep quiet about what you've heard. Do that, and you'll always be our first choice when we need your kind of expertise. Ignore me at your peril."

"Anything else down in that hole?" the ME said to the tech.

"Just some rubble and other trash."

"Let's get it all up here. Remember, photographs first."

With no sign whatever that the tech found the ME's reminder irritating, the guy picked up the blue bucket and carried it back to the well.

Conrad stepped up to Lindsey. "Lieutenant, the boy has been down there for more than fifty years. He needs to be with his family. I'll take financial responsibility for the interment, but I'd like to get this done as soon as possible. How long before you can release the remains?"

Lindsey looked at the ME, who lifted his chin toward Conrad and said, "Who exactly *is he*, again?"

"One of the folks who helped find the boy."

"You a relative?" the ME asked, speaking directly to Conrad for the first time.

"No, just a concerned citizen who wants to see the right thing done."

"Here's the problem… I'm not completely satisfied that we've established the identity of the deceased." He raised a hand as to ward off the anticipated objection Conrad would make. "I know… there's a picture of a boy the right age wearing the same kind of button we found." He glanced at Lindsey. "I'd like a copy of that photo by the way." Then back to Conrad, "But even with it, I want another piece of corroborating evidence… dental x-rays, for example."

"I have no idea if the boy's dentist is still alive," Conrad said. "And even if he is, he probably wouldn't have records from that long ago."

"It could take a while, but we might be able to get mitochondrial DNA samples from some part of the skeleton… possibly the teeth," the ME said. "Then, if we can locate someone in the boy's maternal lineage, we could compare his mitochondrial

DNA with her. That's how the identity of the Russian Tsar's family was established when their bodies were discovered."

"Are you sure all that is really needed?" Conrad said.

The ME looked at Lindsey. "In light of the legal ramifications that seem about to ensue, I'd think you'd be siding with me on this."

Lindsey considered the ME's comment, then said, "I do agree. About that DNA... could you get a usable profile from embalmed tissue?"

"You thinking of exhuming his mother?" the ME said.

"Just explorin' possibilities at this point."

"Embalming fluid cross-links the DNA and makes it unusable for profiling. So that's not the way to go. Put some men on it... check out area dentists and do a genealogy search."

Lindsey nodded. "Later today, I'll see when we could begin doin' that. With luck, it'll be sometime before fall."

This sudden delay made Conrad furious. From the sound of what Lindsey had just said, it could take months to get the ME what he wanted. *Wait a minute...* "You don't need a genealogy search. The victim has a living sister. She's at the Oakmont home. You could get a mitochondrial sample from her."

"That's what we should do then," the ME said. "We might have to ask the Oakmont governing board for approval first, especially if the sister isn't capable of giving informed consent."

"Suppose that works out," Conrad said. "How long before all the testing would be complete?"

"This isn't a TV show," Lindsey replied. "Our state DNA lab is backed up like a dog groomer's sink, and this wouldn't even be considered a high priority case."

"Give me a time frame."

Lindsey rubbed his chin, then said, "Two maybe three months, with luck."

"Sometimes, unrelated individuals can have similar mitochondrial DNA," the ME said. "So I'd actually like to see a match with more than one known relative in the maternal line."

Shit! Conrad thought. *To have come so far and now be blocked by a system that had been a hindrance even when the crime occurred was intolerable.* He looked at Ann and Nate. "I have to go somewhere and think." Then he wandered away, heading back down the path that had now been well worn by all those who'd come there today.

Without their leader, Ann and Nate followed. Not wanting to crowd him while he thought, they hung back and didn't speak.

When Conrad reached Ann's yard, he dropped onto the grass and lay on his back, one forearm over his eyes. He remained that way for over a minute, while Ann and Nate milled around waiting for him to speak.

Finally, he sat up and said, "I'm not ready to let the ME and the state police handle things from this point forward without us. Who knows *when* they'll get around to looking for that second relative the ME wanted. Maybe *we* could find an appropriate person using one of those genealogy sites on the net, and then... I don't know... locate a private lab to do the testing, if that would even be permitted. Within reason, I'd be willing to pay for it myself."

"I've actually had some experience with genealogy searches," Ann said. "Think Lieutenant Lindsey would mind?"

"Mind what... Carrying out his work *for* him? Do it. If he gets upset, I'll tell him to blame me. Meanwhile, I want to check out a long shot idea I have about dental x-rays."

"What can *I* do?" Nate asked.

"I hate telling you this," Conrad said, "but you should probably stay of sight. Those goons who were trying to stop us from finding out what Leathers did—"

"Should now leave us alone," Nate said.

Conrad winced and took a breath to speak.

Noting his reaction, Nate said, "Now that the cops know everything, why would they continue to harass us?"

"Actually, I think that means Ann and I are in the clear. But you're an eyewitness to what happened. If you aren't around to testify, that could help Leathers a lot. So until they catch those guys, watch your step."

"How exactly would I do that?"

"I'm guessing Daddy Rain might have some ideas. You will go see him, won't you?"

"Absolutely. What are you thinkin' about dental x-rays?"

"Let me give it a try before I say anything more."

27

THIS TIME, WHEN Conrad reached Doc Marshall's mailbox, he didn't leave his car on the road, but turned down the long, dusty driveway. He hadn't called ahead because he didn't know the number and couldn't find it. He wasn't worried about the rifle the doc met him with on the previous visit because they seemed to have parted on good terms, even though Marshall *was* muttering to himself as Conrad left.

Making any kind of mistake when it comes to firearms is always to be avoided. The sudden appearance of Doc Marshall on his porch *with* the rifle underlined that principle in Conrad's mind when his car was still about twenty yards from the cabin. An exclamation point was added when Marshall fired the gun into the air.

Conrad stopped the car, shut off the engine, and got out.

"I thought that was probably you," Marshall shouted. "Seein' as how nobody else has been out here in years. Just turn around and leave me alone."

"I only came to ask you one question," Conrad shouted back.

"I been depressed ever since you left. No more reminders needed about things that can't be changed."

"Believe me, I know what you mean."

"I don't think you know *anything* about the subject."

Conrad hesitated. Every day he tried not to think about his role in Claire's death, and every day he failed. Reliving it in his mind was horrible enough, but what he was facing now was worse. And he couldn't do it. He'd admitted his guilt to Ann, but that was a private conversation in which they were exchanging confidences. To shout it to Marshall across such a distance would make it even more real than it was, would shame him under the open sky. Exposure like that was more than anyone could expect of him.

He got back in the car and reached for the ignition key. Then he sat there, thinking. Were his feelings more important than his quest to help the Camerons? What did his views on privacy matter compared to stopping suffering that might continue into eternity if he didn't act like a man?

He opened the car door and slid out. "My wife, Claire, died in a car accident six months ago," he shouted, well aware of how his voice carried, most likely even to the other side of the lake. "And it was my fault. She was going to help rebuild someone's home that had burned down. I was supposed to go with her, but I was too busy. So she went alone and took a route I would not have chosen if I'd been with her. The car hit a slick spot in the road, careened out of control, and..." He was out of breath from shouting, so he paused and stared at the ground, embarrassed and once again angry at himself for what he'd done to the only woman he'd ever love.

Finally, he was able to go on, the rage now showing in his voice. "So you're not the only one in the world who has regrets. Other people are living with them too."

Getting control of himself, he continued, "We think we've found Felder Cameron's remains. If that's true, the whole story of what happened to him can be settled, and he can be buried in the Cameron family plot with his mother and father. I believe that then, even in death, his mother's broken heart can be mended. All we need now is to find some evidence that will convince the medical examiner that the bones we've found are truly his. Dental x-rays could prove it. I came only to ask if you knew which dentist the family used. If you care about the Camerons as much as you say and you know the answer to my question, you'll tell me.

Nothing will make you forget the pain you carry because of the past, but you can do something *now* to help them."

He was once again out of breath from shouting, and his throat felt raw. So he might not have been able to make himself heard if he had to resume his argument. But that apparently wouldn't be necessary, because Marshall put his gun on the porch railing, came down the steps, and walked toward him.

"Their dentist is dead," Marshall said, when he reached Conrad. "Been gone twenty years. Never sold the practice far as I know, so those x-rays are probably under 10 feet of the county landfill. But you don't need them."

"Why not?"

"Felder had an anomaly in the roof of his mouth… a harmless bony prominence known as a torus palatinus. It's fairly common in adults, but not in children. It comes in different shapes… sometimes multilobed… sometimes flat. Considering the rarity in kids and the different subtypes, it can be nearly as good as dental x-rays in determining identity. Felder's was tri-lobed. Did the skull you found have that?"

"I don't know, but I'm already certain the remains we've discovered are his. Now, I just have to convince the medical examiner."

"He may want a signed statement from me about what I've told you. Come back to the porch, and I'll get one for you."

Conrad followed Marshall to the cabin and sat on the porch steps while the old doc went inside.

A few minutes later, Marshall reappeared carrying a folded sheet of paper. As he handed it over, he said, "You got what you came for, now leave."

The old man remained on the porch and watched his unwelcome visitor walk away. Before Conrad reached his car, Marshall shouted, "You're right, this isn't going to make me forget anything about what an incompetent shit I was to Beryl. Hope you have better luck with your memories."

❦

THE LONG CONVERSATION Lieutenant Lindsey was planning to have with Leathers turned out to be quite short because Leathers immediately lawyered up and demanded to be charged or allowed to go home. Since Leathers' lawyer was, even now, still hundreds of miles away, Lindsey had let the congressman go, but sent two troopers along to keep track of him.

At the moment, Lindsey was on the phone in Sheriff Rogers' office. He was listening carefully as the ME responded to what Conrad had learned from Henry Marshall about Felder Cameron's skull. In front of the desk, Conrad, Ann, and Nate waited expectantly to hear the news.

"Okay doc, I'll let 'em know," Lindsey said, hanging up the phone. He looked at the three occupied chairs. "Says he'll release the remains Monday mornin'. But not to any of you directly... only to a rep from a licensed funeral home."

It was finally going to happen, Conrad thought. *No more false hope. This was the real thing.* "Can't we have them any sooner?"

"As long as they been missin', a few more days won't matter."

Inwardly, Conrad replied, *If you only knew the truth, you wouldn't believe that.* What he said was, "Then I better get busy making arrangements."

He went to the office door and opened it, allowing Ann and Nate to precede him. Before they left, Lindsey said, "I'd love to hear the real story of how you all came together on this, because I don't think you've told me everything. For now, I've got enough to deal with, so I won't press you about it. But someday..."

Out in the street, Conrad looked at his two comrades. "Being a writer, I'm a professional liar, so it must be one of you two that gave us away to Lindsey." He didn't actually smile after saying that, but Ann thought she saw a sparkle in his eyes that she'd never seen before.

"Rogers didn't believe us either," Ann said. "And Nate wasn't there. So I guess I'm the problem."

Ann had tried to capture the light in Conrad's eyes and hold it a moment longer with her response, but it vanished like a dream upon waking.

"Nate, that day you put the fence around my garden... I thought you were acting kind of peculiar. You knew where it came from didn't you?"

"I was pretty sure it was from the cemetery, but when you said Claire made you buy it, I figured everything would be okay."

"We have to get it back where it belongs."

"I'll start on it right away."

"I want to help. Let me take care of arranging the interment, then I'll meet you in my garden."

Speaking to Conrad, Ann said, "There's something else that needs to be done. Before you arrived today, Lindsey said no one's spoken to Janine yet about any of this. She should be told that we've found her brother. I can do it."

"I should be there too," Conrad said. "Nate, I'll join you as soon as I can."

❦

"JANINE, I'VE BROUGHT Mrs. Neville and Mr. Green to see you again," Roni Ellison said.

Janine looked at the group from her worktable, where she was making yet another of her paintings. Ann went over and stood close to her.

"Dear, I just wanted to tell you that we've found Felder, and we know everything that happened."

Her face remaining expressionless, Janine turned and looked at Ann.

"It was your last painting that gave us the clue we needed. It's all right now. He's not missing anymore."

Janine's eyes began to glisten. Then a tear formed in her right eye and ran down her cheek.

28

"AMEN."

The minister conducting the graveside ceremony threw a handful of dirt into Felder Cameron's grave. Though it was a small sound, the clatter of the particles as they hit the wicker casket Ann had chosen rang in Conrad's ears like cannon fire. He'd found himself unable to participate in choosing the casket, the whole activity bringing back too many dark thoughts. But it was his idea to attach a baseball bat and a cap bearing a Yankees' logo to the lid. Though the ME had wanted to keep the metal pin for evidence, he finally relented, so Felder's keepsake remained with him.

Conrad stepped forward and handed the minister an envelope containing the required honorarium.

Despite the vigorous gossip mill, the time of the event had been successfully kept from everyone in town except the minister, the two workmen from the T. S. Sherman Funeral Home, and those who had a right to be there. Of course, Conrad, Ann, and Nate were present... and Lieutenant Lindsey. Roni Ellison was there too, only because Janine needed supervision. In keeping with her odd affliction, Janine was calm, but kept her back to the proceedings. Henry Marshall attended as well, but stood significantly away from everyone else and spoke to no one.

Late last week, after the trip to tell Janine her brother had been found, followed by an emotional session at the funeral home, Conrad had helped Nate finish taking the fence down from around Claire's irises. By then, there hadn't been enough time left in the day to reinstall the enclosure at the cemetery. So they had stacked it against the back of Conrad's house under an awning and gone to the Cameron family plot, where they weeded it and mowed the wild growth around it.

Early the next morning, the rain had begun... a generous downpour that fell intermittently for the next four days, not only delaying reinstallation of the fence, but causing the funeral to be rescheduled. However, it did not prevent Conrad from driving to Memphis to find a Yankees' cap. During that drive, he couldn't help but wonder if this was a Daddy Rain crop-watering event, gone sideways, though all the evidence indicated Daddy had full control of everything he did.

The rain had moved on early Monday night, and today had dawned clear and cloudless. This morning, while the grave diggers prepared Felder's final resting place, Conrad, Nate, and Ann had reinstalled the fence, including repainting the section left behind by the thieves when the fence had been stolen.

"You three should be proud of yourselves," Lieutenant Lindsey said, from behind them as they left the funeral and headed for their vehicles.

"Not the emotion I'm feeling," Conrad said over his shoulder. Ann and Nate responded with something similar.

"Yeah...," Lindsey said. "Poorly worded, but I think you understand my sentiment. Look... there have been some developments you need to know about... if you have time... even if you don't, we should go back to the office and talk."

29

ONCE AGAIN, CONRAD, Ann, and Nate were in chairs arranged in a semicircle in front of Lindsey's desk. At the moment, nothing was being said. Lindsey just sat, looking at each of them in turn, nodding slightly as though their expressions somehow verified a thought he harbored.

Finally, when the silence became uncomfortable, Conrad said, "What's going on, Lieutenant?"

"Thought we should discuss some things."

"Like what?"

"Last week, when Leathers' lawyer got here, the three of us spent some time together. Not bein' the kind to take advice from anybody, even if he's payin' for it, Leathers ignored his lawyer's advice to say nothin'. First thing he did was change his story of what happened the day Felder Cameron died. In his new version, he said it was all an accident... that Felder lost his balance and fell into the well while he was leanin' over to see into it. In that new account, Leathers' glasses fell off while he was tryin' to help Felder. Said he made up the other story because his father had forbidden him to play in Bailey Acres and he didn't want to admit he'd been there."

"That's just not true," Nate said.

"Medical Examiner agrees with you. The new story didn't square with damage he found on the side of the skull opposite the lethal fracture. His observations suggest, as you said, that Felder was struck by a hard object when he was on solid ground."

Lindsey looked at Conrad. "Leathers might have kept to his new version, but after our meetin', my men were able to track down the goons who beat you up. One of the thugs admitted it, and said Leathers hired him."

"How'd you find them?" Conrad asked.

Lindsey shook his head. "Doesn't matter. Point is, with that new evidence, Leathers came up with a third account, one he swears is the truth."

Lindsey shifted his attention to Nate. "In this new story, he agreed with everything in your account, right up to the part where you said he killed Felder. He didn't go along with that, because he didn't hit the boy."

Nate shook his head in disbelief. "Who did then?"

Lindsey looked at each of the three sitting in front of him. When the wait became unbearable, he said, "Janine Cameron."

In synchrony, Conrad and Nate said, "What!" Ann sat in shock.

Lindsey continued, "He said she burst out of the weeds and hit the boy in the head with a bottle." He pointed at Nate. "Did you actually see the fatal blow struck?"

Nate sat back. For the next few moments, he didn't respond, but he looked very uncomfortable. Then he said, "I saw Leathers straddlin' the boy, and I saw him put the body in the well, but... no, I didn't actually see the other part. I had to take a... you know... Had to go real bad. So I moved off aways, did my business fast as I could, and went back where I could see again."

Lindsey continued. "When Janine hit the boy, Leathers remembers screamin' at her. Nate, you recall hearin' him say, 'Why'd you *do* that?' "

Nate shook his head, trying to shed all the years that were clouding the past. "It was so long ago... I don't *know*."

"Not really important," Lindsey said. "Last week, after you all left the scene, the ME's tech went back down in that well. He brought up a coke bottle with hair and old blood dried on it. It was caught in a vine tangle about five feet down. I sent it to our fingerprint lab in Jackson, where they got right on it. Anyway, they found some prints from Leathers and others that belonged to Janine. I asked around and apparently her affliction often comes with a violent side."

"Why did Leathers at first hide her involvement?" Conrad asked.

"She wasn't really the Cameron's birth daughter. They adopted her. She was actually the daughter of Beryl's sister. After the sister's husband ran off, the sister committed suicide. Janine had no place to go then, so the Camerons took her in. The way Leathers tells it, Janine was illegitimate, probably why her real mother's husband left her."

"Who was her father?" Ann asked.

"Grady Leathers' daddy. Grady was apparently the only one who knew that. He'd seen 'em together and overheard things. Made him ashamed. He didn't want anyone else to know his father was that kind of man. When Janine killed the boy, Grady figured there'd be a big investigation and with all eyes on Janine, it'd come to light who her father really was. He couldn't allow that, so he hid the body in the well."

"Jesus," Conrad said. "Grady was only six years old and already had a mind capable of that kind of duplicity."

"Born politician," Lindsey said. "Oh… and you were right about Penn Rogers and Marshall Leathers conspirin' to hide what happened."

Conrad shook his head. "Boy, you hear about small town secrets… but this…"

"What will happen to Janine?" Ann asked.

"Considerin' she was clearly mentally ill when she killed the boy and is already in a psychiatric institution, the state's attorney sees no point in prosecutin' her."

"I think somewhere in her broken mind, she's sorry for everything and wanted the boy's remains to be found," Ann said. "That's why on our first visit to see her she kept pointing at the well in her paintings. Then, when we went back to tell her we found Felder, she cried."

Nate stood. "Lieutenant, I'm sorry I said I saw *everything* that happened. I was just so sure about it all, it seemed like I had. Am I in trouble?"

"Why would you be?"

"Sheriff Rogers said because I never told anybody about what I saw, I could be prosecuted for obstruction of justice."

"There's no law that says someone who witnesses a crime bein' committed has any legal obligation to report it. Rogers was probably just tryin' to get you to be quiet."

Letting out a sigh of relief, Nate dropped back into his chair.

"What about Leathers?" Conrad asked.

"That's a different matter. State's attorney is willin' to overlook him hidin' the body because he was just a kid. But those goons he hired to beat you up… that's assault. He's gonna have to stand trial for that. Now, how about you all get out of here and let me get back to workin' on my report for this mess."

30

CONRAD PULLED INTO the driveway of a neat bungalow. Nate must have seen them arrive because he came out of the house immediately, hurried to the car, and climbed in the back seat.

"Ready for this?" Conrad asked, looking at the rearview mirror as he backed into the street.

Nate tapped his chest. "My heart's beatin' so hard I can't get my breath."

"Mine too," Ann said.

"Weather should be ideal," Conrad said. "No clouds to obscure the moon."

"I've never been out this late before," Ann said. "The streets are practically empty."

They rode awhile in silence until Nate touched Conrad on the shoulder. "I just had a thought. How we gonna get in. I think they lock it up at night."

"All taken care of," Conrad said.

A few minutes later they approached the back service gate of the Glenwood Springs Cemetery, and Conrad brought the car to a stop.

"See, that's what I was worried about," Nate said, pointing at a big padlock illuminated in the car's headlights.

Conrad got out and approached the lock. Producing a key from his pocket, he quickly released the shackle, freed the locking chain, and swung the gate inward.

"Where'd you get the key?" Nate asked as Conrad got back behind the wheel.

"Rented it from the owner."

It didn't seem right to go onto the grounds with headlights blazing, so after they passed through the gates, Conrad turned them off. This meant they continued down the narrow asphalt service road, tombstones on the periphery sliding by in dim relief, now lit only by the three-quarter moon and the car's daytime running lights. They drove two minutes in silence, then Conrad stopped and shut off the engine. "I don't want to get any closer than this with the car. It's almost time, so we need to hustle. Be careful and don't slam the doors."

By "almost time," he meant it was a few minutes before 1 a.m.

There were no lights in the cemetery, but it was possible to see reasonably well by the glow of the moon. With Conrad in the lead, they set off on foot across the grounds, the surrounding tombstones vague obstacles to be carefully avoided.

Soon, they reached the gate to the old section where the Cameron family plot was located. There, Conrad paused and whispered, "The best place to watch and not be seen is at the top of the wall. When the time comes, stay as well hidden as possible. Let's go."

The eight-foot high wall surrounding the old area was covered in fieldstone with occasional small stones set horizontally so they extended several inches from the wall, creating little steps. The top of the structure was crenellated like a castle parapet. Conrad led them to a spot on the left, about ten feet from the gate, where the protruding stones were fairly numerous. Then he turned to Ann and whispered, "This is a good place for you. Can you get up there?"

"I think so."

"Then let's get moving. We don't have much time."

He waited until Ann was up the wall and in place, then he and Nate found locations for themselves. Thus, at 12:59 a.m., they were all properly positioned so they could each see the Cameron family plot and still stay hidden by peeking through an adjacent crenellation.

As the seconds crawled by, the crickets that had stopped chirping when the three intruders had arrived, slowly returned to work. Their chorus quickly increased in number and intensity until the sound enveloped Conrad like something he could touch.

Suddenly, as if they had practiced it, the insects all stopped chirping at the same instant.

Conrad now focused so hard on the Cameron family plot thirty yards from the wall that it felt as if his eyes were beetling from their orbits. Without the crickets' song to mask it, he became afraid that the thumping rhythm of his heart hammering against his chest would carry across the grass and ruin the moment.

But then, with moonlight reflecting off him, Felder Cameron materialized from the night and began crying, standing outside the fence, each hand gripping one of the uprights.

Conrad forgot to breathe, and he sure as hell wasn't going to blink.

Inside the fence, a glowing female figure in a long golden gown appeared. She leaned down and lifted her son into her arms. Then, she slowly raised her eyes. Looking directly toward where Conrad and the others were hiding, she put one hand to her mouth and blew them all a kiss.

In the next instant, mother and child vanished.

31

BACK IN THE CAR, the three friends sat speechless at what they'd just seen. Finally, Ann said, "That was a sight I'll never forget."

"I feel like my whole life was leading up to this," Conrad said. "And it wouldn't have happened without both of you. Thank you for that. I just wish…"

"What?" Ann asked.

"Nothing." He looked over his shoulder at the back seat. "How are you doing, Nate?"

"Don't think I really know."

※

WHEN CONRAD GOT HOME from the cemetery, he went into his bedroom, turned on the lights, and walked to the window overlooking the garden, the wondrous event he'd seen less than a half hour ago, still seared in his memory.

Then, *Oh my god…* Though he'd been keeping his computer in sleep mode since Beryl's first message, he heard the sound it makes when it powers up from complete shutdown. He was being summoned!

Deliriously excited to see what was about to happen, he dashed to his study, where he saw the cursor at the top of a new Word page blinking… blinking…

Surely there was more coming. There must be.

The first words began to appear: MY DEAR CONNIE,

Connie! Beryl wouldn't call him that. He felt an overwhelming surge of euphoria wash over him. But he fought it… afraid to let it have him, because he might be wrong. More words came and he dropped into his chair to read them.

YOU'VE DONE A FINE THING FOR PEOPLE WHO COULDN'T HELP THEMSELVES. BERYL IS AT PEACE NOW. AND YOU SHOULD BE TOO. IT WASN'T BERYL WHO ASKED YOU TO HELP. IT WAS ME. I DIDN'T WANT YOU TO KNOW I SENT THE FIRST NOTE BECAUSE YOUR DECISION TO HELP HAD TO COME FULLY FROM YOUR OWN HEART. BY CHOOSING THE WAY YOU DID, I KNOW NOW YOU ARE TRULY SORRY FOR LETTING ME GO OUT ALONE THE DAY OF MY ACCIDENT. CONTINUE TO BE THE MAN YOU'VE BECOME AND I'LL ALWAYS BE CONTENT.

The cursor stopped moving. *No… That can't be the end… She was here… Is she gone…?*
New words began to flow across the screen.

I'VE STAYED CLOSE TO HELP BERYL AND WATCH YOU, BUT NOW I HAVE TO GO.

Go… He instantly hated the word. Elation was replaced by fear.
ONE DAY WE'LL SEE EACH OTHER AGAIN. HAVE NO DOUBT ABOUT THAT, BUT DON'T LONG FOR THAT TIME. REMEMBER ME, BUT ALSO REMEMBER TO LIVE YOUR LIFE FULLY WITH NO REGRETS.
I LOVE YOU.
CLAIRE

Then the words all disappeared, leaving behind only that damn blinking cursor.

A primitive sound that could have come from some wounded prehistoric animal erupted from Conrad's throat. He put a hand on each side of the computer and shook it. "Claire... Don't leave. I need you. Can't you stay?"

But all that remained on screen was the blinking cursor. Conrad moaned again. "I can't make it without you. Claire... Come back."

But she didn't return.

Maybe if he typed it. With shaking hands, he attacked the keyboard. COME BACK... COME BACK... COME BACK...

Nothing.

He shot to his feet, shoving his chair away from him, and dashed out of the room.

⁓

FLASHLIGHT IN HAND, Conrad rushed up to Daddy Rain's porch and pounded on the door. After a long wait, Daddy answered fully dressed.

"My wife," Conrad said, emotion and salty tears clogging his throat. "She just spoke to me... Sent me a note on my computer. Said she has to go... to move on. Help her stay. I know you can do it. Please."

Daddy Rain put a hand on Conrad's shoulder. "Son, her unfinished business here is at an end. Her door is closin' now, and even if I could stop it, you don't want that. You want her to find peace. Let her go. That's what she needs now."

Conrad stared at the old man. The crazy thought that he could somehow force Daddy to help galloped through his frazzled mind. Conrad then dropped his chin in defeat, stood that way for a few seconds, and slowly nodded.

⁓

BACK FROM HIS VISIT to Daddy Rain, Conrad sat at his computer, looking at the framed photo of Claire beside it. He ran his finger over the image as though he could once again feel her downy skin, but all he touched was glass. Suddenly exhausted, he folded his arms on the desk and lowered his forehead onto them. He remained that way until a distinct tug on his ear caused him to leap to his feet.

Claire…?

He spun around the room, looking for the source of the pull he'd felt… but he was alone. His eyes fell on the computer screen. Words were again marching across it:

CONNIE,
THANK YOU FOR UNDERSTANDING. WRITE
YOUR BOOKS, LOVE AGAIN, AND BE HAPPY.
CLAIRE

Not wanting to lose this message, Conrad made a screen shot of it. As the capture software recorded the message with the sound of a camera click, the original disappeared.

❈

NEXT DOOR, ANN Neville, still awake, sat at her kitchen table turning the pages of a scrapbook that contained many pictures of her deceased husband, some with her in them, some without.

❈

NATE GOODRICH GENERALLY found it awkward to sleep with his arm around his wife. Tonight, it seemed the right thing to do

❈

OUT IN THE CABIN by the lake, Doc Marshall dozed in an armchair, the plaque bearing his MD degree lying in his lap.

❈

AT OAKMONT, JANINE Cameron slept peacefully, not sitting up in bed as she had each night for half a century, but lying on her side. On her work table was a new and completely different painting.

-✤-

BEHIND HIS MANSION GATES, Grady Leathers paced the floor of his study, yet another glass of Jim Beam in his hand.

-✤-

IN HIS COMFORTABLE HOME just outside Batesville, Lieutenant Lindsey stood in the door of his eight-year-old son's bedroom, thinking how on Saturday he'd take the boy fishing.

-✤-

BACK AT TRELAIN, Conrad stared out his bedroom window and looked toward Bailey Acres. Claire had said he should love again.

Love again.

What a preposterous thought.

How could she believe that would *ever* be possible?

-✤-

DOWN THE STREET in the house across from Ann's, the lamp beside Roni Ellison's bed was on. In its glow, she read the last sentence in *Pressure Point*, sighed, and closed the book. Then she turned it over and studied Conrad's author photo for at least 30 seconds before setting the book aside and turning off the light.

-✤-

CONRAD RETURNED TO the study, where Claire's final message was displayed in the screen shot he'd kept of it.

WRITE YOUR BOOKS

He sat down, picked up her picture, and pressed it against his chest.

Eventually, he put the photo back in its usual place, got up, and began to pace.

WRITE YOUR BOOKS

He took his seat in front of the computer and navigated to his unfinished and long overdue novel. But he didn't open it. Instead, he just stared at the title.

On impulse, he opened a new Word file and began typing furiously:

The whip-poor-will that had been calling all evening from Bailey Acres packed it in around eleven o'clock. But the cricket jam session in the garden outside Conrad Green's open bedroom window went on until exactly 1 a.m. Then, as if responding to the stroke of a conductor's baton, the insects fell silent...

NOT THE END

"Every man must find for himself the path through grief."
Anonymous

About the Author

D.J. (DON) DONALDSON. Don is a retired professor of Anatomy and Neurobiology. His entire academic career was spent at the University of Tennessee Health Science Center, where he published dozens of papers on wound healing and taught microscopic anatomy to over 5,000 medical and dental students.

He is also the acclaimed author of eight forensic mysteries and five medical thrillers.

He lives in Memphis, Tennessee with Oliver, his West Highland terrier.

"Donaldson is a master of the Gothic mystery." - *Booklist*

Also by D.J. Donaldson

Cajun Nights

Young and vibrant New Orleans criminal psychologist Kit Franklyn has just been assigned her most challenging case yet—a collection of victims with similarities that include driving old cars, humming nursery rhymes, committing murder, and then committing suicide! Welcoming the help of her jovial boss, chief medical examiner Andy Broussard, the two set out to solve the case, devising strictly scientific possibilities. Not once do they consider the involvement of Black Magic, a New Orleans cultural staple, until an ancient Cajun sorcerer's curse surfaces with an ominous warning: "Beware the songs you loved in youth."

NEW YORK TIMES BOOK REVIEW — *His writing displays flashes of brilliance... Dr. Donaldson's talent and potential as a novelist are considerable.*

WASHINGTON POST BOOK WORLD — *Suspensful... likeable protagonists... Broussard and Franklyn are an engaging team... a welcome debut.*

HOUSTON POST — *A deadly portrait of this steamiest of Southern cities... mighty fine.*

MEMPHIS COMMERCIAL APPEAL — *A novel of creepy suspense.... It won't be easily put down, through your heart races to dangerous levels... a face-paced thriller that deserves a wide audience.*

THE PHOENIX REPUBLIC — *Donaldson has relieved the tedium of the murder mystery grind with this engaging tale.*

BOOKLIST — *We close this remarkable, intoxicating book like a first-time visitor leaves New Orleans: giddy, a bit disoriented and much less confident in our own assumptions about life.*

Blood on The Bayou

New Orleans's plump and proud chief medical examiner, Andy Broussard, and his gorgeous assistant, criminal psychologist Kit Franklyn, set off to investigate a series of violent murders. Examination of the victims leads to the discovery that each has the throat ripped out as though they'd been attacked by something inhuman. 'Blood on the Bayou' is written in Donaldson's unique style: A hard-hitting, punchy, action-packed prose that's dripping with a folksy, decidedly southern, sense of irony. Add in Donaldson's brilliant first-hand knowledge of forensics and the sultry flavor of New Orleans, and the result is first class forensic procedural within an irresistibly delectable mystery.

LOS ANGELES TIMES BOOK REVIEW — *The bayou atmosphere is redolently captured…*

BOOKLIST — *Donaldson combines an insider's knowledge with a real flair for making the reader's skin crawl.*

MEMPHIS COMMERCIAL APPEAL — *It's hard to beat his combination of cool science and explosive passion in the heart of humid Louisiana.*

No Mardi Gras for The Dead

Kit Franklyn, lately drowning in personal doubts about her life and career, thinks that investigating the corpse she found in the garden of her new home will be the perfect distraction. Together with her boss, the loveable and unconventional chief medical examiner Andy Broussard, she sets out to solve this case that's growing colder by the minute. Though they identify the body as a missing hooker, now dead for twenty seven years, all hope of conviction seems lost—until the unorthodox duo link the body and two recent murders to a group of local, wealthy physicians.

PUBLISHERS WEEKLY — *Likable protagonists, abundant forensic lore and vivid depictions of colorful New Orleans and its denizens...*

WASHINGTON TIMES — *Kit... and Andy make a formidable team.*

BOOKLIST — *Donaldson's genre gumbo keeps you coming back for more.*

MEMPHIS COMMERCIAL APPEAL — *No mystery has ever started in a more clinically riveting and elegantly horrifying style... If you haven't met Broussard and Franklyn, you should make your introductions.*

New Orleans Requiem

It's a bizarre case for Andy Broussard and Kit Franklyn. A man is found in Jackson Square, stabbed, one eyelid removed and four Scrabble tiles with the letters KOJE on his chest. Soon, there's a second victim, also stabbed and missing one eyelid, but this time with only three letters on his chest, KOJ. The pattern is unmistakable, but does it mean there will be two more victims and then the killer will cease, or is he leading up to something bigger and deadlier? Broussard and Kit use their disciplines to profile the killer, but it soon becomes clear that the clues and objects they've found are part of a sick game that the killer is playing with Broussard; a game most likely engineered by one of the hundreds of attendees at the annual forensics meeting being held in New Orleans. Has Broussard finally met his match?

PUBLISHERS WEEKLY — *Lots of Louisiana color, pinpoint plotting and two highly likable characters... smart, convincing solution.*

NEW ORLEANS TIMES — *An accomplished forensic mystery. His New Orleans is worth the trip.*

JACKSON MISSISSIPPI CLARION-LEDGER — *Andy and Kit are a match made in mystery heaven.*

MEMPHIS COMMERCIAL APPEAL — *Nicely drawn characters… plenty of action and an engaging descriptive storytelling style… An investigation you'll be thrilled to make.*

BOOKLIST — *Donaldson is a master of the gothic mystery.*

KIRKUS — *Ingenious… This is one for those who like their lab talk down and dirty.*

Louisiana Fever

Andy Broussard, the plump and proud New Orleans medical examiner, obviously loves food. Less apparent to the casual observer is his hatred of murderers. Together with his gorgeous sidekick, psychologist Kit Franklyn, the two make a powerful, although improbable, mystery solving duo. When the beautiful Kit goes to meet an anonymous stranger—who's been sending her roses—the man drops dead at her feet before she could even get his name. Game on. Andy Broussard quickly learns that the man carried a lethal pathogen similar to the deadly Ebola virus. Soon, another body turns up with the same bug. Panic is imminent at the threat of a looming pandemic. The danger is even more acute, because the carrier is mobile, his identity is an absolute shocker, he knows he's a walking weapon and… he's on a quest to find Broussard. And Kit isn't safe either. When she investigates her mystery suitor further, she runs afoul of a cold blooded killer, every bit as deadly as the assassin searching for Broussard.

PUBLISHERS WEEKLY — *Delivers… genuinely heart-stopping suspense.*

KIRKUS — *Sleek, fast moving.*

NEW ORLEANS TIMES — *Broussard tracks the virus with a winning combination of common sense and epidemiologic legerdemain.*

BOOKLIST — *This series has carved a solid place for itself. Broussard makes a terrific counterpoint to the Dave Robicheaux ragin' Cajun school of mystery heroes.*

JACKSON MISSISSIPPI CLARION-LEDGER — *A dazzling tour de force… sheer pulse-pounding reading excitement.*

MEMPHIS COMMERCIAL APPEAL — *(A novel of)* *"terrifying force…. utterly fascinating… His best work yet.*

LOS ANGELES TIMES — *The autopsies are detailed enough to make Patricia Cornwell fans move farther south for their forensic fixes. … splendidly eccentric local denizens, authentic New Orleans and bayou backgrounds… a very suspenseful tale.*

DEADLY PLEASURES — *A fast moving… suspenseful tale. Andy and Kit are quite likeable leads… The other attraction is the solid medical background against which their story plays out.*

KNOXVILLE NEWS SENTINEL— *Vivid crisp writing… If your skin doesn't crawl with the step by step description of the work of the (medical) examiner and his assistants, it certainly will when Donaldson reveals the carrier of the fever.*

MERITORIOUS MYSTERIES — Donaldson paints the Crescent City with the vivid hues of summer while evoking the autopsy rooms of Gray's Anatomy. His protagonists meanwhile, are those you'd like to invite to dinner.

Sleeping With The Crawfish

Strange lesions found in the brain of a dead man have forensic pathologist Andy Broussard stumped. Even more baffling are the corpse's fingerprints. They belong to Ronald Cicero, a lifer at Angola State Prison… an inmate the warden insists is still there. Broussard sends psychologist Kit Franklyn to find out who is locked up in Cicero's cell. But an astonishing discovery at the jail and an attempt on her life almost has Kit sleeping with the crawfish in a bayou swamp. And Broussard, making a brilliant deduction about another murder, may soon be digging his own grave.

KIRKUS — *Streamlined thrills and gripping forensic detail.*

MEMPHIS COMMERCIAL APPEAL — *With each book, Donaldson peels away a few more layers of these characters and we find ourselves loving the involvement.*

BOOKLIST — *Cleverly plotted top-notch thriller. Another fine entry in a consistently outstanding series.*

SAN ANTONIO EXPRESS-NEWS — *The pace is pell-mell.*

BENTON (AR) COURIER — *Exciting and realistic. Donaldson… starts his action early and sustains it until the final pages.*

MERITORIOUS MYSTERIES — *The latest entry in a fine series which never disappoints.*

Bad Karma In The Big Easy

Andy Broussard, the plump and proud New Orleans medical examiner, obviously loves food. Less apparent to the casual observer is his hatred of murderers. Together with his gorgeous sidekick, psychologist Kit Franklyn, the two make a powerful, although improbable, mystery solving duo. Among the dead collected in 'The Big Easy' floodwaters after hurricane Katrina are three nude female bodies, all caught in the same brush tangle, none with water in their lungs. No water. Broussard knows this was not an act of God; not the work of Katrina. There's a killer on the loose and by God, Broussard means to find him. But Broussard has perhaps the biggest challenge of his colourful career. The city and all its records are destroyed, practically the entire population is scattered, the police force has no offices and many of the rank and file (who haven't defected) are homeless. And if that's not bad enough, Broussard discovers that the bodies were all once frozen solid, completely obliterating key forensic clues. Soon, Broussard and Franklyn are on a dangerous and labyrinthine journey through the obscenely damaged, ever mysterious, irresistibly seductive, city of New Orleans; leading them to a kind of evil that neither of them could imagine.

ONCE UPON A CHAPTER — *I immediately fell in love with Donaldson's characters. They fit so well together it was like a family. I enjoyed Bad Karma in the Big Easy so much, I'm going back and picking up the first six books in the series.*

GLENDA BIXLER, BOOK READER'S HEAVEN — *I love this series... one of the best writers in this field... surprising... and horrendous!... brought me to the edge of my seat...*

ALEXIA PURDY BOOKS — *I couldn't stop reading... many twists, turns, and surprises... kept me flipping each page... rich detail... raw, descriptive... incredibly real. A great introduction to an intricate storyteller.*

J BRONDER BOOK REVIEWS — *A great book in a wonderful series. Mystery/thriller readers, you HAVE to read this book.*

Assassination at Bayou Sauvage

Andy Broussard, the plump and proud medical examiner for the City of New Orleans, is sitting almost in the kill zone of a too-close-for comfort and 'in living color' murder of his Uncle Joe Broussard at a family picnic in Bayou Sauvage - the largest urban wetlands park in the USA. Surprisingly, the murderer then immediately commits suicide. After easily determining the killer's identity from the driver's license in his pocket, the only remaining task for Broussard and the police is to uncover the motive for such a heinous act. But suddenly, everything about the case takes a bizarre turn. Caught short handed because of an NOPD work slow-down, and needing someone to find out what happened to a young woman who has just been reported missing, Homicide Detective Phil Gatlin deputizes Broussard's beautiful death investigator, Dr. Kit Franklyn, and assigns her to that case. Shockingly, Kit's efforts soon lead back to the murder of Uncle Joe. Sensing a plot of horrendous magnitude, Broussard directs his colleagues and friends in a race to uncover the truth behind the most audacious Andy and Kit mystery of the entire series.

D. J. Donaldson's fans can rejoice once again, knowing that Kit, Andy, Phil, Bubba, Grandma O, and Teddy are back in a terrific new story that pushes their abilities to the limit.

TESS GERRITSEN — *D.J. Donaldson is superb at spinning medical fact into gripping suspense. With his in-depth knowledge of science and medicine, he is one of very few authors who can write with convincing authority.*

READERS' FAVORITE — *This gripping murder mystery with explicit crime scenes and gory details will captivate the reader and keep them on the edge of their seat until the shocking and unexpected conclusion... realistic and electrifying. Blood, guts, and chills abound in this jolting thriller.*

THE BOOK WORM CHRONICLES — *...deeply engrossing, audacious. The setting totally made me feel like I was there. Great read.*

WRITER'S THREAD — *The characters are memorable and easily jump off the pages and dance with the reader, while both the setting and the plot line have enough twists and turns to keep even the most die-hard mystery fanatic guessing.*

Thanks for reading! Dingbat Publishing strives to bring you quality entertainment that doesn't take itself too seriously. I mean honestly, with a name like that, our books have to be good or we're going to be laughed at. Or maybe both.

If you enjoyed this book, the best thing you can do is buy a million more copies and give them to all your friends… erm, leave a review on the readers' website of your preference. All authors love feedback and we take reviews from readers like you seriously.

Oh, and c'mon over to our website:

www.DingbatPublishing.ninja

Who knows what other books you'll find there?

Cheers,

Gunnar Grey,

publisher, author, and Chief Dingbat

δ

Made in the USA
Coppell, TX
26 April 2020

21532634R00108